To Ally

Bruce
and
the Road
to
Honesty

Gale Leach

by Gale Leach

TWO CATS PRESS
Surprise, AZ

Bruce and the Road to Honesty
Copyright © 2012 by Gale Leach

Cover design by Elizabeth Engel. Book design by Gale Leach.
The text is set in Palatino Linotype; headings and cover type
are set in Gabriola.

Published by Two Cats Press, Surprise, AZ

ISBN-13: 978-1-937083-37-3
ISBN-10: 1937083373

For information about special discounts for schools or bulk
purchases, please contact Two Cats Press:
623-810-5044 or info@twocatspress.com.

For Morgan, Scott, and Travis
with all my love

Acknowledgments

I am grateful for the help I have received from my family and friends, especially my husband, Richard, whose wonderful sense of humor made its way into these pages.

Thanks to Dr. Karl Klook, of Cal State, Bakersfield, who provided interesting and useful information about scorpions.

Thanks to Rebecca Valbuena and her fifth-grade students, whose enthusiasm for Bruce and his friends gave me inspiration to continue their journey into this book and beyond.

Finally, thanks to my editor and friend, Jim Campbell, who worked his magic with my words and made this book better.

Contents

Chapter 1

The Ceremony

Bruce checked himself over again and straightened his feelers for the umpteenth time. His smooth, green skin shone. He took a deep breath and let it out slowly. It was time.

All of his family had gathered around and were talking about his changing. Ceremonies like these were always large events, bringing family members and friends together for the happy occasion. Bruce was a little embarrassed at having so much attention, but he was also proud to be doing something that had once scared him so much. He thought back to the time, not so long ago, when the idea of changing from a caterpillar into a butterfly made his stomach turn upside down and his skin get all tingly. Now his skin was tingly again, but it was because the time of his changing was nearly here, and he was ready.

His family was not large. Unlike most butterfly households, his parents had only made one egg—his egg. Most other caterpillars had dozens of brothers and sisters and aunts and uncles. Looking around, Bruce could count the members of his family without using any of his legs twice. Grandpa Walter was there, of course. Aunt Bess and Uncle Howard had flown over, too. There were also cousins, aunts, and uncles

1

he didn't see very often but who cared enough to join him as he began his transformation. Milton was there, too, and he'd said he would stay until Bruce emerged from his chrysalis. Thinking about that, Bruce smiled, wondering again how this friendship between a caterpillar and a spider could have happened.

Bruce was brought out of his reverie as Aunt Bess began running her forefeet over his shoulders, telling him not to be afraid and that it would be over before he knew it. Bruce made a crooked smile and answered "um hum" several times in response to her questions and comments. Looking around, Bruce saw his father talking with Grandpa Walter. He waved his arms a bit, hoping one of them would come and free him from Aunt Bess, but no luck. He looked the other way and saw his mother. He gave her a small wave and was relieved when she lifted off the ground and flew toward him. Bruce watched as she flitted this way and that, and he thought that his mother was still the most beautiful butterfly he'd ever seen. She landed behind his Aunt, nudging Bess until she stopped talking and turned around.

"Bess, would you mind checking on the raspberry dessert? I think it might be done now."

With a nod and a smile, Bess wandered away. His mother glanced at Bruce and then looked in his father's direction, nodding just a little. His father and grandpa flew over and landed near his mother. Bruce didn't like the serious looks on their faces.

"Arlene, did you . . ." Bruce's father's voice trailed off.

"No, not yet," his mother said, twisting her forefeet together.

"Bruce, I know you're excited to begin, but your mother and I want to talk with you for a moment before the ceremony starts. Besides going over the usual traditions for your changing, we need to tell you something . . . something we probably should have told you a long time ago but never found the right time."

Bruce had no idea what they meant, and he just stood looking at his parents. A long, awkward silence settled over them, until Grandpa Walter snorted and said, "For goodness' sake, Henry, get on with it. You can't wait any longer."

Bruce was more puzzled than before. He hoped it wasn't something bad. His father's feelers were twitching—a sure sign that he was upset.

"Ahem. Well, yes," his father said, now twisting his front feet together. "Your mother and I have tried to find the right way to tell you this for a long time. For all of your life, in fact." He paused. When the silence hung there and Bruce didn't say anything, he continued, "We can't let you begin changing without explaining how you came into this world. You need to hear the story of how we found your egg."

Bruce couldn't believe what he'd just heard. "You found my egg?"

"Yes!" Bruce's mother piped in, moving forward to help his father who was obviously having difficulty explaining this. "We were so excited! We had tried and tried to make our own eggs, but we never had any luck. One afternoon, your father and I were out flying, and we noticed a small, round object lying in the grass. I flew down and realized it was an egg. Your egg. I couldn't leave it behind. Neither of us had ever seen

3

an egg like it before, so we knew it couldn't belong to any of the butterflies of our village. I didn't care where it had come from—I picked it up and flew home with it—with you—and tended it until you hatched."

Bruce was still trying to absorb what he'd heard. He stood unmoving, looking back and forth between his parents.

His father spoke again. "Bruce, what we're telling you is that we don't know what kind of insect you will become when you change. You may be a butterfly . . . or you might be a moth."

At that, several of Bruce's family members who were eavesdropping drew in a breath, like a collective small gasp. Bruce became upset. His family had no idea what moths were really like, and he thought it was stupid for butterflies to think less of them. He was about to say so when his mother spoke again.

"Of course, it doesn't matter what you are, at least not to us. We love you, and we will always love you. We were so happy to have found you, and we're glad you are our son. You've made us complete in a way we never could have been without you." She paused and looked down at her feet. "I'm sorry we didn't tell you sooner. We tried so many times! We could never find a way to do it properly, and whenever we decided to tell you, something came up, and it didn't seem to be the right time. I hope you understand. We never meant to hurt you."

Bruce looked at his parents and aunts and uncles. His thoughts were all jumbled up. He looked at Grandpa Walter, concentrating on his wrinkled face and legs and his wings that were faded because he was so old. Bruce wondered if he would even have wings after he changed. What if he became something else entirely? What if he wasn't even a moth? His eyes pleaded with Grandpa Walter for answers. His grandpa was the oldest butterfly in the village. He had to know something, didn't he?

Sensing Bruce's need for reassurance, his grandpa said, "I don't have many words of wisdom, young one, other than these. Your parents love you. That's more than a lot of young creatures can say. You can count yourself lucky for that. They took in your egg and cared for you. They chose you. That's something special. Whatever you may become, it won't matter. Who you are won't change, and all of us will still love you. Your parents may have been wrong to wait so long to tell you, but even parents aren't always perfect. We do the best we can, and that's what I expect of you now. You're my grandson, and I love you. Stand tall, and be as brave, as you always are."

Bruce felt numb, like his head had been cut off from the rest of his body. His feelers wiggled this way and that, but his legs were heavy, and he felt like crying. He wanted to go away, lie down, and curl into a ball.

Milton walked toward his friend. The fact that the jumping spider didn't somersault in the air or bound toward Bruce indicated that he felt serious, as well. "You're having an adventure right now, you know. It's a bigger adventure than you thought it would be, but you've been through things that were harder than this. You're lucky to have parents and family who love you. Seeing your family and how much they care makes me a bit homesick. After your changing, maybe we can try to find my family so I can introduce you to my parents and brothers and sisters." Milton placed his foreleg on Bruce's shoulder. "But your mum's right: this family is special. They chose you, and they'll love you, no matter what."

"Mom—Dad—I can't believe this," Bruce said, ignoring Milton's words and still feeling confused. "You found my egg on the grass? What did it look like? Where did it come from? Did you ever try to find my real parents?"

Bruce's mother turned her head away, and his grandpa spoke quickly. "Bruce, these are your real parents. They didn't create your egg, but they are your parents because they raised and loved you as their own."

"Yes, but I want to know where I came from. I want to know what I really am. I might be a moth," he said, as if he were chewing a bitter leaf, hoping to get a reaction from his cousins, "or maybe even a beetle larva or a glowworm!" He enjoyed the whispers and titters that statement caused among his family members. "I can't change unless I know what I'm going to be when I wake up!"

Bruce's mother looked like she might cry, and his father's antennas twitched fiercely.

"I don't think . . . you're a glowworm," his mother said, sniffing. "Your egg was green like you are, and shiny. It was a very pretty egg, and I certainly don't think you're a beetle larv—" She turned toward Henry and buried her head in his wing. He raised a forefoot and wiped a tear from her eye.

Bruce knew he was acting badly, but he was upset, and he felt he had a right to be hurt. His mother and father shouldn't have kept this from him. They should have known that he would want to know about his egg parents—who they were and where they lived. Perhaps they didn't tell him because they were afraid he would leave. Maybe they cared more about having an egg of their own than about his feelings.

Now he knew for sure that he needed to find his egg parents.

"Mom, I'm sorry, but you and Dad should have told me. Sooner, I mean. I can't change without knowing what I am—what I'll be. You shouldn't have hidden this from me—that wasn't fair. And now you tell me, just before I'm ready to become a ... something ..." He shook his head. "Milton—you want to find your family again, right?"

Milton nodded, but he looked sad. "Bruce, think about ..."

"What I think is that we should pack. We'll go find your family and look for my egg parents at the same time. Once I know for sure what I'm going to be, I'll come back and let all of you know," he said, gesturing at his relatives who were staring at him. "Then, if you still want to have a ceremony—if you still think of me as one of your family—I'll change. But I have to go now. I have to know."

"If you feel that way, you should go," Grandpa Walter said harshly. "You're being selfish and unappreciative. Your parents—these parents—have given up much to raise you. Until today, I thought they'd done a good job. I'm ashamed of your behavior. Perhaps this journey will give you answers, but I don't care whether or not you find your egg parents. I hope this trip helps you find some manners and common sense."

Even seeing Grandpa Walter so angry didn't change Bruce's feelings. "We'll leave in the morning," he said to Milton, who nodded slowly. "Right now, I need some time to think."

Bruce turned and walked toward his home without looking back. Milton swayed from side to side. When he spotted a leaf bug that landed not far away, he headed in its direction. Bruce's other relatives mumbled to themselves and began flying away. After a little while, Bruce's parents joined them, sighing as they flew home.

Chapter 2

Leaving Home

Bruce woke up and shivered. He shook his head to rid his thoughts of the horrible dream he'd had. In the dream, he'd made his chrysalis and had emerged only to discover that he was a dung beetle. Not liking that, he'd made another chrysalis, only he turned into a cockroach. Just before waking, he dreamed that he tried again and came out as a centipede.

He was exhausted. Not a good way to start a new journey. It was still dark now, but it would be light soon. He pulled out his backpack—the new one his mother made after his other was lost in the bat cave—and walked to their eating area. He was filling his pack with tender leaves and was startled when his mother appeared out of the shadows.

"I thought you might come and get supplies before you left. I couldn't bear you leaving without saying goodbye this time, so I waited for you."

"You've been here all night?"

His mother nodded and looked down at her feet.

Bruce dropped his pack and moved to where his mother stood by the wall. He reached out and hugged her, and she stroked his face with her forefeet.

"I'm sorry about yesterday. I know I hurt you.

9

But I still don't want to change until I know who or what I am. Do you understand?"

She nodded and backed away a little, smoothing the edges of her wings with her feet.

"I'll be back soon. My egg couldn't have traveled very far on its own, could it? My other parents have to be somewhere nearby. We'll find them, and we'll find Milton's home, and then I'll come back. Milton's been away from home for a long time, and he's really homesick." Bruce knew he was exaggerating about Milton's feelings, but he thought his mother would feel better about his leaving if it was for Milton, too. "I'll say goodbye to Dad before I go. If I can send word about how we're doing, I will." He saw a tear forming in his mother's eye and leaned over to kiss her. "I love you, Mom."

She smiled, brushed her tears away, and reached out to hold his front feet in hers. "I love you, too, Bruce. Promise me you'll be careful."

"I will."

Bruce took the pack and walked toward his parents' sleeping area. He found his father awake, too.

"So, you're ready to go," his father said, gesturing at the backpack. His tone was gruff.

"Yes, sir. I came to say goodbye."

"Don't go without saying goodbye to your mother."

"I already did." Bruce shifted his weight from side to side.

"Well, I suggest you look for someone who can give you more information. How about those moths you stayed with—Angie's parents? Maybe they would know where your egg came from. I'd start by going there, if I were you."

"That's what I thought, too. If they don't know, maybe they'll know where I can find out. After that, Milton and I will look for his parents. Once we've done that, I'll come back."

"Then I'll see you when you come home." Bruce reached out to shake his father's forefoot, but his father rose, walked toward Bruce, and held him in a strong embrace. When he let go, Bruce was red in the face but glad for the hug.

"I love you, Dad. I . . ."

"You need to get this over with. Your changing will be better when you get back. Now, go—and the two of you be safe. Tell Milton I want him to watch out for you, and you for him."

"I will," Bruce said, and he headed out of the house before he could change his mind.

He saw Milton in the distance, hiding behind a tree trunk. Something was flying near him, darting back and forth in the air. Then Milton was in the air, too. When he landed on the ground, the dragonfly he'd been stalking was clamped firmly in his mouth. It didn't take long before Milton dropped the remnants of the creature and noticed Bruce. He bounded over and somersaulted, landing right in front of him.

"Are you ready? I'm excited to be going on an adventure again. Is everything okay with your parents?"

"Yes, I'm ready to go."

"Did you apologize?"

Bruce scowled. "Everything's fine. After you," he said, sweeping his leg in a grand gesture in the direction of the road.

Milton somersaulted, and the two of them started walking the way they'd come not so long ago. They avoided the pavement that now covered the road and stayed along the edges on the dirt. Bruce hoped this journey would be easier than their last one. How hard could it be to find their families?

Chapter 3

The Moth Village

hey made it to the outskirts of Angie's village as it was starting to get dark. Bruce still thought it strange to see so much activity in the evening, since his village began getting quiet at sundown, and he and his parents seldom went out at night. But moths were nocturnal—as the sun was going down, they were waking up and starting their "day."

One of the moths flying by recognized Bruce and Milton and let out a cry. "Hey, everyone, come out! Bruce and Milton are back!" The moth flew toward the center of the village, calling to everyone as he went.

Bruce and Milton continued walking toward Angie's home. More and more moths and caterpillars showed themselves, rubbing their eyes and smoothing their feelers to shake off sleep. Angie's youngest brother was the first to come out from their sleeping area, and he jumped up and down when he spotted them. Seeing this, Milton jumped up and down, too, until both of them were bouncing in unison, trying to see who could jump the highest. Finally tired from the exertion, the young caterpillar sat down and fell over on his side, panting. Bruce started to laugh out loud when he was tackled from the side. He fell over as Angie hugged him, and when she let go and moved back, it looked like she was waiting for him to say something.

"Um, hi, Angie," Bruce said, turning red. "How are you?"

"Oh, Bruce, it's so good to have you here, but I thought I wouldn't see you until after you changed. I'm almost ready to change myself. Did you just come to visit or can you stay until my ceremony?"

"No, we didn't come to visit. Well, yes, to visit, but no, actually to ask questions. And to visit. But we can't stay for the ceremony, I don't think. We're here mostly to ask questions." He stopped and took a deep breath, trying to compose himself. "Is your father here?"

"My father? Yes, but why..." Angie stopped in mid-sentence. "Never mind. I'll get him." She scampered off toward her sleeping area. It wasn't long before a handsome moth followed her out.

"Bruce!" Angie's father said, holding out his forefeet so that Bruce could touch them with his own. "It's good to see you, but we didn't expect you so soon. Now I'm curious. Angie says you want to ask me some questions?"

"Milton and I came here trying to find our families." Seeing the perplexed look Angie's father gave him, Bruce realized he would have to start from the beginning. He explained about his parents telling him they'd found his egg, about wanting to find his egg family, and that Milton wanted to find his home again, too. "Can you tell me if you—I mean, your caterpillars—come from round, shiny green eggs?"

"No, our eggs are oval and white. We have some cousins whose eggs sound like those you've described, but they live far from here. I doubt any of their eggs could have ended up that far away."

Bruce found he'd been holding his breath, and he let it out in a long sigh. He hadn't realized until now that he'd hoped Angie's father would say yes and that his search would be over. It wasn't going to be that easy. "I guess we'll have to keep looking."

"Not tonight, young ones," Angie's mother said, as she flew over and landed near them. The air from her wings raised a little cloud of dust.

"Oh, I'm sorry for that. I'll be happy when the rains come again. This dryness makes it so difficult to keep everything clean. But never mind that. Come dine with us and rest before you go anywhere. You and Milton are always welcome, and we'll enjoy getting caught up on what's been happening with you and your family."

Bruce knew there was no point in arguing with Marta, so he and Milton joined the moths for their first meal of the day. Marta's food was delicious, and Bruce ate more than he probably should have. When the meal was done, he and Milton and Angie went walking together. When they reached the edge of their village, Angie suggested they sit and talk. She described what she'd been doing since they'd seen each other last, and some of her stories made Bruce and Milton laugh. But as she was about to finish a funny story, she saw that Bruce was leaning against a tree trunk with his eyes shut, and he was gently snoring. Angie gestured for

Milton to follow, and she led him to a sleeping area where he would be safe.

"Good night, Milton. Have a good sleep."

"Good night, Angie. Thanks. It's good to be with friends again."

She smiled and went back toward her home to begin her day with her family.

Chapter 4

The Journey Begins

In the morning, Angie's family feasted again. Her mother had made small packages for Bruce and Milton to take on their journey, and Angie's father took them aside as they were packing to leave.

"I don't know if it will do any good, but you might inquire with the great owl at Stony Ridge and see if he can guide you in your search. He is old and quite wise, they say."

"The owl at Stony Ridge?" Bruce said, his voice quite high. "We can't go to see him. He'd eat us!"

"Oh, that's just stories parents tell their young ones when they want them to stop doing something or be quiet. Large owls rarely eat insects as small as we are. Only the smaller owls do that. Also, if you visit in the morning, the owl will most likely have eaten during the night, and you wouldn't look terribly tempting. Mind you, he might not know anything that will help. However, he's lived here for years, and everyone says he's the wisest creature around."

Bruce thought about it as he finished packing his bag. "Thank you, sir. If we can't find anything else along the way, we'll definitely think about talking with the owl." But even as he said it, a small chill ran down his back. The owl at Stony Ridge had been so much a part of his nightmares as a young caterpillar that it was hard to think of him any other way.

Bruce hoped they might run into the pigs again. They seemed to know a lot about what was happening around them, and they might have seen eggs like his before. If that didn't happen, he would have to be bold and ask others they met along the way. Eggs didn't travel on their own, so his egg parents had to be nearby.

When they had packed everything Marta had given them, Angie appeared with a little more. Bruce smiled and made room in the already full backpack for the tasty milkweed leaves and the rose petals. She had even gathered some nectar in a pouch made from another leaf, but Milton decided that was too good to save, and he slurped it up on the spot.

"I have to start eating less or else develop more muscles," Bruce said, lifting the bulging pack onto his back.

Angie smiled and touched him on the shoulder. "I hope you find your egg parents, Bruce. I don't know how I'd feel if I'd been adopted, but when you find them, I hope that . . . well, I hope you like them."

"Me, too." Bruce leaned forward and hugged Angie, and then he touched forefeet with Angie's father. He reached toward Angie's mother, but she flew to Bruce and gave him a big hug.

Bruce looked at Milton and pointed back up the road leading away from Angie's village. "Are you ready?"

"I'm always ready!" Milton said, bouncing a

little again. The sun's rays filtering through the trees illuminated the hairs around his body, making him look somewhat comical, and Bruce giggled.

"If you need the old owl," Angie's father said, "I've heard he makes his home in the huge oak tree about two days' walk up the road. You can't miss the tree. It's in the middle of a clearing with grass and shrubs. Just make sure you visit in the morning after he's had a chance to hunt during the night."

Bruce and Milton thanked Angie's parents and began walking toward the road. Angie waved when Bruce turned around, and he waved, too. Then everyone was waving, and Milton turned two somersaults. This continued until they had moved out of sight of the village.

The going wasn't difficult, but, as the sun rose higher in the sky, Bruce found himself getting hot due to his heavy load. At lunchtime, they sat and rested beneath the shade of an apple tree. Bruce set his pack down and began munching a crunchy leaf—a new taste that Marta had included in her sampling for him—and Milton darted this way and that, chasing flies. He knew that Bruce didn't mind his eating other insects. While their friendship demanded that they treat each other differently than they would other bugs, it didn't mean they had to deny their nature.

When Milton had eaten enough, he snuck behind Bruce and made a silent jump. When Milton landed right beside him, Bruce dropped the leaf he was eating, lost his balance, and fell over onto his side. Milton was very pleased and began humming to himself, looking around as if nothing had happened.

"Don't do that! I hate it when you do that!"

When Bruce got to his feet, he was mad, but then he realized Milton had played a joke on him, and he was secretly pleased.

Milton pretended to be busy licking juices from his forefeet and grooming the hairs near his mouth. "Do what? I have no idea what you're talking about. Are you ready to go yet?"

"I'm going to get you for this. Just wait!" Bruce hid his smile as he picked up his pack.

"Let me carry that for a while. At least until you have your senses about you. Imagine being scared of me. I wouldn't hurt a fly. Well, then again, maybe . . ." Milton tossed the pack onto his back. He couldn't get his legs into the straps, but he wound some of his silk through the openings and fastened that around his midsection, which seemed to work quite well.

They headed out again, walking and jumping along the side of the road, staying as much under cover as possible. As the day went on, Milton passed the time by telling Bruce about his family and the place where he used to live. Bruce didn't say much. The walking was getting harder because they'd started climbing. He realized that Stony Ridge was probably quite a bit higher than his home. As the road climbed, Bruce kept thinking about his awful changing ceremony, finding his egg parents, and all the other things that now consumed his thoughts. He nodded automatically when Milton said something that needed his response. He began wondering what he would do when he found his egg parents. He knew that, no matter how many different ways he might imagine that first meeting, the real event would be different. Finally, he gave up thinking about it and started listening to Milton and asking questions about his home.

Bruce kept a lookout, but so far they hadn't seen many birds, and nothing else had bothered them. Thinking of birds made Bruce recall the first time he flew on Meryl's back during their last adventure. He was terrified, being so afraid of heights, but getting to the cave quickly to find Angie and the others was a stronger need, and he managed to do it. Bruce knew it was going to take longer on this trip without Meryl to fly them where they were going, but he thought back to Meryl's words again: "If it's worth doing, it usually takes hard work to get it done." Bruce sighed. He wasn't against hard work, but he thought having things easy wouldn't be that bad, either.

When evening came, both he and Milton were both tired. They chose a large nut tree to protect them as they settled down for the night. Milton found some loose bark that he used to create a shelter in a small hollow made by the tree roots, and they made their camp there. After Milton hunted and Bruce ate more of the delicacies from his pack, the two lay together, curled up near one another, as that helped to keep them warm.

While trying to sleep, Bruce decided that, if they didn't find anyone who was able to help them tomorrow, he would go to the huge oak to visit the owl. He shivered again and tried to think of other things. Angie came to mind. He settled into sleep thinking of her, while Milton was already snoring a little.

The next day, they walked nearly all the way to the

clearing, and they didn't meet the pigs or anyone else who could give them any useful information. By late afternoon, they saw the huge oak tree and continued toward it, being careful to stay out of sight. Bruce's fears of the owl from Stony Ridge were huge, and he found himself constantly looking around to see if they were being watched.

The oak tree stood in the center of the clearing, just as Angie's father had described. A few bushes and some grasses grew in clumps here and there, but there wasn't much to give them cover there. Bruce decided they should get as close to the huge oak as possible without leaving the shelter of the trees outside of the clearing and make camp there for the night. In the morning, when the owl would have eaten, they would creep through the clearing and up to the tree. What they would do after that was further than Bruce cared to plan.

Chapter 5

The Owl at Stony Ridge

hen he awoke, Bruce saw that fog had settled over the entire area. The sun was up, and it was light enough to see, but the fog gave an eerie, closed-in feeling to the place, and the clearing that had appeared so open and huge was nearly invisible.

Bruce touched Milton's shoulder and shook him awake. Milton sat up, looked around, and said, "What did you do with the trees?"

"Your snoring must have attracted this fog."

"What snoring? I don't snore."

Bruce snorted.

"See—you're the one who snores," Milton said, stretching each of his legs, one after the other. He stood and looked around. "It's going to be hard to find flies in this, but I'll give it a try." He attached a silken thread to the trunk of a tree behind them. " I'm setting a line here so I'll be able to find my way back if I can't see you. I won't be gone long," Milton said as he walked away into the fog.

It was eerily quiet with Milton gone. Bruce took a wild raspberry leaf out of his pack. Besides being juicy, the leaf was covered with many short hairs that tickled his mouth.

When he'd eaten as much as he could, he sat and waited for Milton to return. A long time went by, but there was no sign of him.

"Milton? Hey, Milton. Are you out there?"

No response.

He called again. Still nothing.

After as much time as he could bear sitting alone, Bruce stood and tried to see something, anything. The fog was too thick. He moved forward and touched the line that Milton had fastened to the tree. His mind was busy conjuring all kinds of ideas. What if something had happened to Milton? He couldn't stand the idea of losing his best friend again. He would find Milton, everything would be all right, and they could get on with talking to the owl. He grabbed his backpack, put it on, and started following the line.

It was sticky, but Bruce discovered he could avoid getting stuck to the line if he touched it lightly. He learned the best way was to touch one of his feelers to the line as he walked along. It was slow going, since the line went in different directions from time to time, and there were rocks and sticks that he had to crawl over. He knew that Milton had simply bounded over these things, and he wished he could jump like that. After he'd walked for what seemed like a very long time, he called out again.

"Milton? Are you there?"

"Bruce, come here! I need your help."

"What's wrong? Are you all right?" Bruce made his way toward Milton's voice as quickly as he could.

"I'm fine, but this little mouse isn't. Come and help."

Bruce followed the line until he could just make out Milton's shape in the mist. He saw a furry lump on the ground in front of the spider and assumed it was the mouse. Bruce wasn't afraid of mice, since they only ate grasses, leaves, and seeds, as far as he knew, but he couldn't think of anything he or Milton could do to help a mouse in trouble.

When he reached Milton, he saw that the mouse was lying on her side in the short grass and the spider was holding onto the edges of a gash in her fur, trying to pinch the wound closed. Her eyes were shut, but she was breathing. She was still alive.

"What can I do?" As he spoke, the mouse opened her eyes and looked at him. Her eyes were round and dark, but they still looked bright as she glanced from Bruce to Milton, or what she could see of him, since he was standing over her.

"Wounds this large need to be held closed so they can heal," Milton said. "I can use my silk to bind the opening shut, but I can't do that and hold the wound closed at the same time. Crawl up on her side, stand over the opening, and squeeze your legs together to keep the wound shut. I'll start wrapping my silk over the wound a little at a time until it stays closed."

"My mom sent some herbs with me. They're in my pack. Do you think they might help?"

"Couldn't hurt. Bring them, and I'll put some over the wound when I'm wrapping it shut."

Bruce pulled the herbs from his pack and climbed up onto the mouse's side. He was surprised at how soft her fur was. From a distance, through the fog, he had thought she was a dull gray color, but up close, she was brown and gray, and she even had small bits of white fur in her ears and behind her cheeks.

Bruce moved under Milton's legs until he stood over the wound. He grasped the mouse's furry skin and began squeezing.

Milton lifted his legs away and smiled when Bruce held the wound closed by himself. "Good," he said. "Now I'll get to work."

Milton let out a little silk and twirled the end of it around his foreleg. He reached up to the start of the gash and stuck the silk to the mouse's fur, making sure he used enough so that it wouldn't come loose. Then he grabbed the line a little further back and stuck that to the other side of the wound. He took a few of the herbs and dropped them over the gash as he continued binding it with his silk. Bruce raised up and moved backward a little after each "stitch," so that Milton could continue his work. When they were done and Bruce stepped away from the gash, it stayed shut, as Milton had hoped.

Bruce climbed down from the mouse, walked around by her head, and watched her breathe. Her eyes were shut again. Although a mockingbird and a mouse are quite different, Bruce couldn't help thinking about the last time he saw Meryl, lying on the ground in another clearing. He hoped this mouse would survive.

"How did you know about closing wounds and using your silk for that?" Bruce asked.

"Remember when we found the orb spiders, and I talked with Dora during our last journey? She told me that humans would come and steal her web sometimes, which made her upset because then she had to spin another. After a while, she learned that the humans use the webs to bind their wounds because the silk makes a covering that holds the wound closed and helps it to heal. Dora said she didn't feel so bad then, but she still thought it was rude that they didn't ask her permission first. Anyway, I remembered that when I found this poor mouse lying here bleeding. I hope she'll be okay."

Bruce looked around. The fog had begun to thin, and he could see more of the clearing now. "We can't leave her out here in the open, or she'll be eaten for sure, but I don't think you and I are strong enough to move her, and that might not be a good idea anyway. Let's find some soft leaves and cover her up. If birds and other predators can't see her, she ought to be safe."

They collected leaves and arranged them over her body in a small pile. When they had placed the leaves just so, with only a small opening for the mouse's face, Milton jumped over and over the pile, from one side to the other, securing his line over it and to the ground so that the leaves wouldn't blow away. While Milton was busy doing that, Bruce gathered seeds and pieces of grass and placed them near her head in case she became hungry.

As Bruce placed the remaining herbs in his pack, the mouse opened her eyes again. "Thank you," she whispered. "I won't forget."

"Rest here until you are better. Get well," Milton said.

"Be safe," Bruce added. Looking at Milton, he asked, "Did you find enough to eat?"

"Yes. I found a couple of beetles and a..." He stopped, realizing Bruce probably didn't want to know the gory details of his breakfast. "Yes, I'm full now. Are you ready for the owl?"

"Ready as I'll ever be." Bruce swallowed, trying to keep his courage up, and started off after Milton who had taken the lead. Milton was still playing out line behind him so that Bruce could follow more easily.

The fog was still there, but it was receding as the sun's rays warmed the air. Standing in the clearing, about halfway to the oak tree, Bruce looked around and saw the tops of the trees behind them and to their sides still vanished into the mist. Looking ahead, all he could see was an enormous brown tree trunk with leaves overhead and more mist.

They continued walking, staying low and moving through the grass and under the small shrubs that were their only cover. It took a while, but they finally reached the base of the tree. It was darker there because of the leaves overhead, and the bark of the tree was covered with moss and lichen. Small mushrooms grew all around. There were also a lot of large, oval objects that seemed to be made of fur and other things. Some of these objects had disintegrated, and Bruce realized they must be from the owl—they were pellets containing the inedible portions of his meals. Bruce swallowed hard, trying not to think about that, even as he recognized some of the remnants as small bones.

He removed his pack and leaned it against the trunk of the tree. He stood as tall as he could and called upward into the leaves. "Hello, m-mister owl from Stony Ridge. Are you there?"

Bruce heard a rustling, but no one answered.

"Hello? Helloooo?" he yelled.

"No need to holler," said a small voice from overhead. The reply startled Bruce, and he ducked automatically. Then he felt silly because the voice didn't sound like an owl, or at least not like he thought the owl should sound. Perhaps he had a cold.

"Sir owl? My f-friend and I have come to ask for your help."

"Ah, more seekers wishing counsel. Well, you've come to the right place. Don't be frightened. You've awakened me now, so give me a moment and I'll fly down to see you better."

Bruce and Milton tried to stand tall as they prepared for the owl to descend. They saw a small shape unfurl its wings, circle around, and land on a branch not far over their heads. This was an owl, but it certainly was not the legendary owl from Stony Ridge his parents had told him about.

This was the smallest owl Bruce had ever seen. He looked just like the larger owls, but he was about the size of an overgrown robin. Bruce wondered if he was supposed to be that little, or if he just hadn't grown.

Bruce tried to be calm. He could see that Milton was nervous, too, as he swayed from side to side and tapped his forefeet on the ground. Owls of any size could be deadly, and Angie's father had said that little ones liked to eat insects. Then he realized this owl had also said they'd awakened him, so that meant he hadn't eaten yet. Bruce gulped.

"W-we came to ask the great owl some questions about butterfly eggs. Oh, and also about a p-place that is over the water from here. Actually, the egg could be a moth egg, and we don't have one with us—an egg, I mean—but we have a description of the egg, and we know it became a caterpillar. I mean, it became me, and I need to know if it—I mean me—is a moth or a butterfly. And the place we're looking for is where my friend here was born and—"

"My goodness, that's enough. Don't be so nervous. Of course, the great owl does eat small animals, as do I—we all have to eat something, don't we? But we receive so many gifts from travelers such as yourselves that we have little need to hunt anymore. In any case, the great owl isn't here right now. I watch over things while he is away, and I'm taking questions in his absence. My name is Conrad. So, now—describe this egg, please."

Bruce glanced at Milton, who raised his forefeet and shrugged his shoulders. Having made up his mind to come here, Bruce felt disappointed that he couldn't talk to the great owl himself, but he thought it couldn't hurt to explain to Conrad what they hoped to learn.

"It w-was a round, g-green egg, about the same color as I am, about this b-big," Bruce said, holding his forefeet apart to show the size.

"Hmm. I'll need to gather more information," Conrad said, blinking his eyes. "Most likely, the great owl and I will have to consult with some other sources, and that may take a few days." He raised one of his talons and began preening his claws, pulling away small bits of hair and skin from what must have been a previous meal. "Of course, you understand that we don't generally provide information without you sharing something in return. Did you bring a gift?"

Bruce's spirits fell. They didn't have anything the owl would want. "We didn't know about that. We don't have anything for you."

"Well, young fellows, you're in luck. You seek information, and I do, too. As a payment for answers, I ask that you retrieve a book that was recently stolen from the great owl. It's a cookbook that contains all of the owl's favorite recipes, collected over many years. A few days ago, a praying mantis took the cookbook, thinking I wouldn't notice. I'd feel terrible if the great owl came back only to find I'd lost this book. I can't go myself, because I promised the owl I'd look after some owlets in a nest nearby. Bring back this cookbook and I will ask the great owl to provide the answers you seek when you return."

"Do you know where the book is?" Bruce asked.

"Yes. I'll give you directions. The book is a little large for you to carry alone, caterpillar, but I think the spider could manage it. I'm sure you'll find a way — that is, if you really want the information."

Bruce wanted answers, and he didn't have any other ideas about how to get them. While he hadn't planned on trading a gift for information, the owl's request seemed reasonable.

Bruce turned to Milton, who cocked his head to the side and shrugged his shoulders. "Do you think we can get this book?" he said quietly, hoping the owl couldn't hear.

"I don't know," Milton said, "but I'm not sure that's the right question. I think we should ask whether it seems like the right thing to do. Can we trust this owl?"

Bruce shrugged. "I don't know, but we don't have any other options, do we?"

Milton sighed. "No, but I think we should be careful. Conrad seems okay, but the hairs on my head tell me something's not right."

"Do you always trust the hairs on your head?"

Milton rolled his eyes. Bruce looked back at the owl.

"If you'll give us whatever information you have about this cookbook, we'll try to get it for you."

"Excellent! I thought you might be the right ones for this job. The praying mantis is a known thief who never tires of stealing things and then telling others they were hers all along. She lives not far from here in a willow tree close to the ocean. I will give you all the details."

"We have another question. It's about where my friend was born."

"Let's deal with one question at a time. For now—relax. I need to ask you some questions so I can be sure the great owl's answers will be those you seek. Then I'll give you more details about the location of the book, and you can be on your way."

Bruce sat down and listened, giving answers when Conrad asked questions. Milton stood, still tapping his forelegs. Bruce knew his friend wasn't comfortable with this task, but what did the hairs on Milton's head know about anything?

Chapter 6

Setting Out Again

"raying mantises eat caterpillars and spiders. On purpose!" Milton swayed from side to side, obviously agitated.

Talking with the owl had made Bruce hungry again. He'd eaten half of an apricot leaf, the rest of which he was now stuffing into his pack. "Look, we won't go near the mantis. We'll make sure she's gone before we go in and get the book. Then we'll bring it back to the owl, and he'll give us the information. It'll be easy."

"I don't know. What if she comes back while we're looking for it?"

"You can stand watch, while I go in and look around. You've got good eyesight. You'd see her coming in plenty of time."

Milton put his foreleg on Bruce's shoulder to stop him from packing. "I don't know. This just doesn't feel right."

Bruce looked at Milton. "It's the only way to get the information. You want to find your family, don't you?" He started stuffing the leaf in his pack again.

"Yes, but I want to be alive when I do." Milton shivered. The wind was picking up, and it whistled through the branches overhead.

"Come on," Bruce said, as he slung the pack onto his back and looked across the clearing. "We've faced worse than this, and we're still here. Let's just get going."

Milton stared at Bruce for a long while and then shook his head. "If I can't talk sense into you, at least let me check on the mouse before we leave."

Bruce nodded, and they retraced their path to where they'd seen her last. She wasn't there, but now there was a trail leading through the grass. Following the trail, they found her sitting up, leaning against the base of a low bush. She had placed leaves around her as Bruce and Milton had done before.

The mouse smiled when she saw them. "That little owl almost got me this time. I owe you my life, little ones."

"It was Milton," Bruce said, pointing to the spider. "He had the idea to use his silk to keep your wound closed."

"I thank you both for your kindness, and I would repay it in time."

"Just keep feeling better," Milton said. He picked up one of the leaves that had fallen from her pile and placed it back over her feet. "Save your strength and get well."

"Do you need more seeds?" Bruce asked. Before she could answer, he began searching the nearby area. He didn't find as many as before, but he also gathered some grass and one acorn. He didn't know if she would eat that, but he figured it couldn't hurt. He placed them next to her on the ground.

"Thank you," she said. "My friends call me Josie,

and I hope you will, too. I heard you say you're going away but will be back later. I look forward to seeing you again when you return."

"We'll look for you, Josie. I hope you feel better soon," Milton said, waving his forefoot. He turned and followed Bruce, who had begun walking out of the clearing.

When they reached the trees, the air was getting colder as the sun sank lower in the sky. They stopped to rest a bit, and Bruce opened his pack again to nibble on a leaf.

"The wind is stronger now, and the leaves are turning upside down," Milton said. "My father told me that means a storm is coming. Why don't we wait here and let it pass?"

"Look, I'm not afraid to go. If you want to stay here, that's okay. I'll get the book myself." Bruce closed the backpack, put it on, and began walking. After he'd gone a short way, he stopped and looked back over his shoulder. "Are you coming?"

Milton didn't answer.

Bruce looked down at the ground. He was silent for a while, listening to the wind in the trees and watching the leaves swirl around his feet. Part of him thought that Milton was right. He knew he should be wary of Conrad and his request, and wary, too, of visiting the praying mantis' home. But the other part of him—the part that still felt hurt by what had happened at his changing ceremony, and the shame of not knowing what he might become—that part wanted to know what he was—who he was—and nothing else seemed very important.

"Milton, I'll do anything to find out what I am—what I will become—and who my real parents are. I'm scared, too, but I don't know any other way to get this information. We can at least try, can't we?"

Milton walked toward Bruce and poked him gently with his forefoot. "We can always try. Let's go."

Chapter 7

Henry

The wind grew stronger as they walked along the edge of the forest. They were following the owl's directions to the willow tree, doing their best to keep out of sight. As they passed close to the side of a small hill, rain began to fall in large, cold drops that plopped around them, making wet circles in the dirt and spattering them with mud.

As the rain increased, Bruce knew that Milton had been right about waiting out the storm, but he didn't mention that, saying only, "We should look for shelter."

"Up there," Milton said, pointing to an opening in the side of the hill. "Looks like that's the only place around."

They scrambled up toward the hole, getting more and more soaked. When they reached the opening, Milton bounded over it to the other side. It appeared to be a small cave. It was getting dark, and they couldn't see inside. Both of them listened and sniffed the air to make sure nothing threatening was inside. When they were pretty sure no predators were there, they both scurried in, almost getting stuck, because the passage wasn't wide enough for both of them at the same time.

Suddenly, they smelled something horrible, and

they both backed out into the rain.

"Aw, you could have done that out here instead of waiting until we were inside the cave! I can't believe you did that!" Bruce said, dodging raindrops.

"I didn't make that stink," Milton said. "I thought you did."

They were surprised to see a small, grayish-brown bug appear inside the opening, looking back at them, blinking his eyes. The bug hung his head. The wind twirled his feelers in circles, and the wind lifted his front feet off the ground, threatening to blow him away. The rain began falling faster, making it hard for the little bug to keep his footing in the watery rivulets.

"I'm sorry. That always happens," the bug said, looking particularly bedraggled as a large raindrop plopped on top of him. "Listen, I'll go, if you want to come in out of the rain."

"Did you make that stink?" both Milton and Bruce asked in unison.

"Yes, but not on purpose!"

"That's a pretty horrible smell," Bruce said. He thought the bug might drown in the puddle that was forming outside the entrance if he didn't move soon. "Is there a cave in there?"

The bug nodded and bowed his head again.

"Well, get back in, but don't stink anymore, okay?" Bruce said as he moved forward and guided the bug back inside as Milton followed.

The space inside wasn't large—Bruce thought it had probably been a small animal's burrow—but it gave them a dry place to stay until the storm passed. The muddy ground near the opening changed to dried mud and then plain dirt further back. As Bruce's eyes adjusted to the darkness, he looked at the space behind him. Seeing no signs of anything to worry about, he began to relax. He shook himself to get rid of the excess water on his skin and was surprised to see that Milton did the same thing at the same time. The little bug got the worst of it, and he rubbed his eyes to get the moisture out of them.

"So, what happened with that smell before?" Bruce asked as he removed his pack.

"I'm a stink bug, but I didn't do it on purpose. It's not supposed to happen unless I want it to. It's my way of scaring off things that want to eat me."

"It sure would do that!" Milton said, making a face but still smiling.

"But you can't control it?" Bruce said.

"No, not very much. Whenever I get excited or scared, out comes the stink. The problem is that I get excited a lot, so it's pretty smelly around me all the time. I used to try to keep it in. I'd squeeze my sides, or I'd try holding my breath, but it never worked. The best I could do was to run away when I felt it coming so that no one around me would know I'd let it out."

"I can see where that would be a problem," Bruce said. He remembered when he didn't have any friends. He thought being a stink bug might be even worse.

"This is my friend, Milton, and my name is Bruce," he said, extending one forefoot toward the bug.

"My name is Henry, but everyone calls me Hank," the bug said, touching forefeet with Bruce. "Well, anyone who actually talks to me does—but that's not a lot of folks anymore."

Milton extended one of his forelegs toward Hank who jumped, and suddenly the horrible smell was all around them again.

"Oh, I'm so sorry," the bug said, cringing. "See— that's what happens when I get scared! Spiders usually eat bugs like me, and it was kind of automatic to . . ."

Bruce's eyes were shut and he was waving his antennas, while Milton danced around in circles, raising and lowering his two front legs. Bruce thought Hank's odor might be the worst thing he'd ever smelled—worse even than the time that skunk sprayed near his home. This smell made his eyes burn, too, and he thought he might throw up.

As the smell began to fade, Milton said, "I'll be careful not to scare you from now on. For now, just believe me when I say that I'm not going to eat you. I can't believe anything would eat you, knowing you made that smell." Smiling, he slowly extended his foreleg toward the little bug again.

"Nice to meet you," Hank said, tentatively touching the tip of his foot to the tip of Milton's hairy leg. "That's a first for me. Making friends with a spider."

"My father's name is Henry," Bruce said. "Don't you like that name?"

"Wasn't me who changed it. It was the other bugs who call me names. You know—'Hank stank, he smells rank,' things like that."

"Yeah, I know," Bruce said. He thought for a moment. "I'm going to call you Henry. It's a good name, and you'd like my father." Bruce was suddenly homesick. He missed his mother's cooking, his warm sleeping space, and the everyday life at his village.

40

Since he'd returned from his previous adventure, it had been really nice to be home. But the memories of the recent ceremony and his father telling him about finding his egg and being adopted made him frown, thinking again that his parents should have told him sooner. He should have known all along.

"I like the name Henry," Milton said. "And there aren't many words that rhyme with it, either."

The little bug smiled, and it transformed him completely. His eyes sparkled and he looked so happy that Bruce wasn't even sure it was the same bug.

"Thank you, both of you!" Henry said. "You're very kind. Before you came along, I didn't care if I never saw anyone else again. I came out here to this cave to live the rest of my life alone, where it wouldn't matter if I stunk or not. But the two of you showed up, and now . . . well, I haven't felt this good in ages!" Henry stood on his back legs and twirled in circles, waving his antennas and his front legs as he danced. Bruce and Milton laughed to see him so happy. When Henry stopped to catch his breath, the three of them sat watching and listening to the rain fall outside the cave.

"Where were you going before the storm came?" Henry said.

"We were looking for a willow tree and a praying mantis that lives there," Milton said, grimacing. "I'm still not sure it's a good idea . . ."

"No, it's a fine idea," Bruce said. "We're doing a favor for an owl who is going to help us in return." Bruce stared at Milton. "We need his help."

"Wow, a praying mantis? That's dangerous,"

Henry said. "I thought praying mantises ate bugs like you."

"They do," Milton said quickly before Bruce had a chance to reply.

"We're not going to get eaten," Bruce said. "We went to a bat cave and dealt with Stang, and along the way a cat, and lots of other things. I'm not afraid of this mantis."

"That's the problem," Milton said. "You should be, and you're not, and that scares me."

"You went to a bat cave? What was it like? What did you do there?" Henry asked.

Milton said nothing and just looked at Bruce. Bruce wasn't sure why Milton seemed to be upset with him. "We rescued a friend of ours and some other bugs who'd been taken by bats."

"Wow! Really? That's amazing. I'm afraid of bats!" Henry became animated and started dancing on his back legs again. "How did you do it? Did you sneak up behind them and . . ."

"Hey, don't get excited or you'll stink again!" Bruce said.

Henry dropped down, looking a little dejected.

"You know, I bet if you worked on it, you could learn not to be so scared," Bruce said. "If you could learn to relax, you probably wouldn't stink as much, at least not when you didn't want to, and you could be with your friends again."

"He ought to come along with us," Milton said. "If he could learn not to stink when facing a praying mantis, most likely he'll have conquered his fear."

Bruce was pretty sure that Milton was being

sarcastic again, but as he thought about what Milton said, he had an idea. "You know, Milton's right. If you did come with us, you would get practice learning not to stink. Of course, if you got really scared, it would be okay if you used your odor, you know?"

Milton's eyes narrowed and he stared at Bruce. "What are you thinking?"

"Just that it might help Henry learn to get over stinking when he didn't want to, and it might help us to have him along if we need to scare away the mantis."

"What if mantises don't have a sense of smell?" Milton asked.

"You're being ridiculous," Bruce said, sighing. "It was your idea, and I think it's a good one. What do you say, Henry? Want to come along?"

Henry looked at Bruce and Milton. "I came to this cave thinking I'd never be with anyone ever again. The other stink bugs hate me. You'd think they wouldn't mind so much, because they're used to the smell. I never had any friends, and I've been so lonely." The little bug stopped talking and sat quietly, looking out at the falling rain. "If you mean it, I'd like to go with you. I'll try hard not to be scared and not to stink—that is, unless you want me to. Do you think the mantis will be very big? How far can they jump? You know, I can jump really far, and I can fly, too. Do you want to see? And I have claws on my feet, and I can use them, when I have to. And I'm not so little anymore. I'm growing, and—"

"Hold on, Henry," Bruce said. "I think it would be fine." He looked at Milton. "It was your idea. Do you agree?"

Milton didn't say anything right away, and the little bug looked very sad.

"That's okay," Henry said, shaking his head. His shoulders sagged and he looked down at his feet. "I understand if you don't want me along. It's no problem."

"Henry, it's not that I don't want you along, but this is going to be dangerous. I don't want you to get hurt."

Henry perked up again. "Oh, that won't happen. I'll be with the two of you, and you fought with bats and cats and rats, well maybe not rats, but bats and cats, and it will be okay, I know it."

Outnumbered, Milton shrugged his shoulders. "Okay. I guess we can give it a try."

Bruce looked satisfied, reached out, and patted Henry on the back. "We'll stay here tonight and leave in the morning, if the weather's clear. Okay?"

"Okay!" Henry said, dancing in circles again. Milton just shook his head.

Chapter 8

Searching for the Cookbook

The rain stopped just before sunrise. After eating, the travelers set out, trying to avoid the puddles that seemed to be everywhere. Some of them were very large, reflecting the clouds and rippling as the wind blew over them. The frogs enjoyed the puddles and were making quite a racket. Bruce took special care to stay away from their croaking, since he knew that frogs loved to eat insects.

Because of the wetness, the going was slower than before, but Henry didn't have any trouble keeping up. Bruce had wondered if that would be a problem. Henry walked slowly, but he was able to jump quite high for a bug his size, and every once in a while, he'd make a huge leap and catch up with Bruce and Milton, or he'd fly a short distance ahead and wait for Bruce to catch up to him. Spying Milton occasionally jumping in the air and landing next to Bruce, Henry decided this was a good game. He started leaping right next to both Bruce and Milton, making them jump, and then he would laugh and laugh. It seemed to Bruce that the little bug was trying to make up for all the times that he'd been sad.

They came to a particularly large puddle, and Milton had an idea. He fastened his silken line to a large, thick leaf near the edge of the water and then he jumped over the puddle to the other side.

"Get onto the leaf and hold on," Milton said to Henry with a smile on his face.

Henry jumped onto the leaf and grabbed it with his claws. Milton began pulling in his line and the leaf skimmed across the surface of the puddle, with Henry squealing in happiness.

When the leaf reached the other side, Henry said, "Let's do it again! Can we do it again? That was fun! Let's do it again, okay?" Henry jumped off the leaf and began bouncing up and down, but then he stopped and stood as tall as he could on his back legs. He gazed into the distance with a strange look on his face. "Look at that," he said, pointing in the direction they were headed.

Bruce looked and saw that the trees thinned out, and now he could see the sky, with its puffy, white clouds. Below that, beyond the ground and the trees and the grass, was an expanse of blue, darker than the sky, like nothing he'd ever seen.

"Is that the ocean?" Henry asked.

The owl had told them that the willow tree was at the edge of a clearing that overlooked the ocean. Bruce had never seen the ocean. He'd heard stories about it—that it was larger than you could imagine, that it went on forever, as far as you could see, with no end. He didn't know how that was possible, but he was excited to see it anyway.

"I think so," Bruce replied, and he began looking around to find the willow tree. Conrad had said they would know the tree because its branches fell downward and many of them touched the ground. He saw the willow ahead of them across the clearing, and he pointed to it. They continued walking, staying close to the edge of the forest, so as to be under cover of the trees. They hadn't seen many predators on their trip so far, and Bruce hoped to keep it that way. He knew that having Milton along was a special help, since he had so many eyes, and he could see just about every direction at once. Still, Bruce kept watch for birds, bats, reptiles, and small animals that might want to make a caterpillar or a spider—and now a stink bug—into a snack.

By the time they neared the willow tree, it was almost lunchtime. Bruce's stomach was rumbling again, and even Milton said he was hungry. He hadn't been taking time to hunt along the way as much as he usually did. Bruce wasn't sure why Milton's behavior was different on this trip, but he figured it would sort itself out eventually. He suggested they take a little while to eat and rest and keep watch on the tree. The others agreed. Milton said he would bring back some leaves and sap for Henry to eat. Henry thought that was a splendid idea, and he waited with Bruce when Milton bounded away into the forest.

"He's nice," Henry said.

"Yes, he is. He's my best friend." Bruce took a leaf out of his pack and handed another smaller one to Henry.

"Thank you. It's strange for a caterpillar to have a spider for a friend, I think, but I can see why you do." Henry began sucking juices from the stem of his leaf. "Yum. The stem's the best part, don't you think?"

"The stem? Actually, I like the leaf part best," Bruce said. "I like the chewiness of these leaves, and the sweet taste they leave in your mouth when you're done."

"I don't chew," Henry said. "I just suck the juices out. So I guess you could eat the leaves and I could suck on the stems. That's good, don't you think?" Henry said, cocking his head.

Bruce smiled. He remembered when Milton used to make him smile on the last trip, and how much he enjoyed that. Now this little bug was doing the same thing. "Henry, Milton isn't the only nice one around here. You're pretty nice yourself. Thanks for making me smile."

"Careful. If you get me flustered, I'll stink again," Henry said with a grin.

The two of them continued eating until Milton came back carrying leaves for both of them. He dropped them in a small pile and brushed his forefeet together. "Good sap in some of those, Henry, and I think they're the kind you like, too, Bruce."

"Milton, the two of us agreed while you were gone that you're a pretty nice guy," Bruce said. "Of course, I shouldn't tell you, 'cause I don't want it going to your head."

"Too late. My head's larger already. See how small my eyes look?" Milton squinted his eyes nearly shut as the others laughed.

Milton suddenly ducked down and motioned for the others to do the same. Bruce dropped onto his stomach and smelled a horrible stench.

"Oh, no, Henry!" Bruce whispered, and closed his

mouth, trying hard to be quiet. He shut his eyes tightly against whatever Milton had seen as well as the acrid smell in the air that made his eyes burn.

"I'm sorry," whispered Henry, and Milton poked both of them lightly to make them be quiet.

They remained crouched and motionless. Bruce wondered if he would get used to the stinky smell if he was around it long enough. He didn't think so. Finally Milton motioned for Bruce to rise up a little and pointed into the clearing.

Bruce stood, opened his eyes, despite the acrid, burning feeling, and looked where Milton pointed. He saw a very large praying mantis climbing down a branch of the willow tree. She carried a package under one foreleg, which didn't seem to slow her down. Bruce watched as she flew from the tree to the grass at the far edge of the clearing. That had to be the praying mantis they were looking for, since she came from the willow tree. They were in luck! Bruce let out the breath he'd been holding and stood a little taller as he watched the mantis walk out of sight.

"If we can get up into the tree quickly, we should be able to go into her home, get the book, and leave before she gets back. This is perfect," Bruce said, smiling.

"I think I should go alone first," Milton said, and he raised a forefoot when Bruce started to object. "I travel faster than you can. Sure, we know that mantis is gone, but what if there's another one up there? If I go, I can check it out quickly. If no one's there, I'll look for the book, grab it, and bring it down, and we can go back to the owl."

Bruce realized that what Milton said made sense, even if he didn't like being left behind. He didn't think there would be another mantis there—he'd heard that female mantises often ate their mates, as well as other insects—but it didn't hurt to be cautious, and all of them didn't need to go. He nodded. Milton took a large jump and set off toward the tree. Bruce was always amazed at how far Milton could jump when he wanted to.

After Bruce gathered the leaves and put them into his pack, he and Henry began walking toward the tree. It wasn't long before they saw Milton reach the hanging boughs of the willow and begin climbing up into the dense leaves up high. They kept watch for the mantis, in case she came back quickly. They hadn't seen anything, when they heard Milton call them.

"We can hear you," Bruce said. "Did you find the book?"

"No, I don't see any cookbook. There are other books—one about gardening, one about—well, never mind. No cookbook, though."

"Did you search under things? She might have hidden it, if it's valuable."

"I did, but there aren't that many places to look. I'll search again, though, if you want me to."

Bruce sighed. He wished he were there and could see for himself to be sure. Yet he believed Milton, so the book must be somewhere else. He'd really hoped they would find it here. Where else could it be? He looked up into the tree again and could make out Milton's shape near the top of the branches. "No, I know you already looked. Come on down."

As he said this, a shadow moved overhead from behind him. He leaned over Henry and held him down, trying to be still to avoid being eaten by whatever was overhead. He was suddenly engulfed in the awful aroma that was Henry's stink. Bruce eyes closed involuntarily, and he forced them open so he could look around and see what had made the shadow. About halfway to the willow tree, he saw an enormous dragonfly hovering in the air. Feeling safe again, he got off the bedraggled stink bug and moved a distance away to let the smell fade away.

"Okay, I'm on my way," Milton said, and started jumping down through the branches. When he was nearly down, Milton leaped to the ground and then saw the dragonfly. He bounded over to Bruce, only to back away again when he recognized Henry's now-famous aroma. "Henry, we really need to work on keeping you calm."

"But he jumped on me!" Henry said, pointing at Bruce. "Why did you do that?"

"I was trying to save your life," Bruce said, frowning. "I saw a shadow and I thought it might have been a bird. I didn't think you'd seen it, and I didn't want you to be eaten. But you're welcome, anyway. I guess I'll let you fend for yourself from now on."

"I think your little friend does that very well," the dragonfly said as she flew closer. "That odor would be enough to discourage even the heartiest of predators from consuming you."

Bruce was fascinated by the dragonfly. He'd never seen one up close before. Her wings beat so fast that it was impossible to really see them—they were only a blur of dark gray. Her body was long and slender, a deep, shiny blue with streaks of black. Bruce marveled at her ability to hover in the air, nearly motionless.

Remembering these flying experiences with both Meryl and Julia, Bruce wondered what it would be like to fly on a dragonfly. He was roused from his thoughts when Henry started jumping up and down.

"I didn't mean to do it," Henry said, his face getting red. "He fell on me!"

"Never mind, Henry," Bruce said. "It wasn't your fault, and we're not upset. But I think Milton's right. We should work on trying to keep you calm, like we planned." Turning to Milton, he said, "Any ideas about the cookbook? What do we do now?"

"Maybe we can find someone around here who— no, wait a minute. The mantis had a package with her when she left. What if that was the cookbook she was carrying?"

"Of course she would have taken her cookbook with her," the dragonfly said, flying closer to Milton. "She is on her way to the competition, and she intends to win the prize."

"What competition?" Bruce asked. "What prize?"

"Why, the great chef's competition. They hold one every year. Animals and insects from all over go to the island to compete, each one hoping to win the prize. It's a great honor, you know."

"What island?" Bruce and Milton said together.

"My, you are full of questions," the dragonfly said, zooming away from them. Bruce thought perhaps she was tired of talking with them, when he realized she was simply hungry: she'd caught a fly. When she had finished eating it, she dropped back down and hovered between them again. "It's clear enough today . . . if you have good eyes, look out there behind me, far out on the water, and you can see the island. Lots of different creatures live there, and many travel between the island and the mainland, where we are now. Birds go there to nest and come back here to live; some turtles do that, too. Other creatures simply travel there for pleasure or for things like this competition. It's a special event because of the pact that the creatures make: no one eats anyone else unless they're on the menu. Now, let me be the nosy one. Why you are looking for the mantis? You know that she will eat you if she gets the chance? You'll be the main ingredients in her next culinary creation."

"Yes, we know that," Bruce said, finding it hard to see the dragonfly in her current position because the sun was directly behind her—she was a black silhouette against the bright sunlit sky. He moved over a little bit to avoid looking into the sun. "But someone told us that she stole the cookbook and he wants it back."

"Perhaps the owl wants it back so he can to go to this competition," Henry said.

"I don't know about any of that," said the dragonfly, "but she'll definitely have the cookbook with her on this trip. You'll have to cross to the island and get it from her there or wait until she returns, and that would not be for many days. Now I must be going."

"You've been very helpful, and we appreciate your kindness," Bruce said, bowing to the dragonfly.

"Ah! A bug with manners," the dragonfly said, dipping her body in a salute to him. "How nice to see that from someone so young. I hope you find your mantis, and I hope you come back with the book you seek without losing your heads." And then, in a flash, she flew beyond the clearing toward the ocean and was gone.

"Do you think we can get to that island?" Bruce asked, looking out toward the speck of land he could barely make out in the distance. It looked very far away. Bruce felt very small.

"Only one way to find out," Milton said. "Let's keep going."

The three of them headed toward the afternoon sun that was sinking closer to the horizon.

Chapter 9

Scorpions

It was getting near sunset, and the travelers were tired. They had decided to keep going until nearly dark, so they would be that much closer to the water the next day. As always, they had kept to the edges of the clearing, close to the trees, but now they'd come to a place where doing that would take them very far around and much longer, whereas going across the clearing would save time. After some discussion, they decided that going across would be worth the risk.

Milton kept a lookout, using all of his eyes that didn't point directly forward to scan the sky, as well as what was on either side and behind him. They came to a spot where there were quite a lot of rocks, large and small, and the going was slower as they made their way around and over these. The light was beginning to fade, and one particularly tall rock stood before them. Milton jumped on it to get a better view of their surroundings. Suddenly, a dark shape crawled out from under the rock into the twilight.

"Scorpion!" cried Milton, and he leaped down, landing in front of Bruce to stop him from coming around the rock and running into the scorpion's outstretched claws. Henry let out a stink and flew back a few feet. The scorpion darted around the rock, his pincers clicking and his tail upraised. Bruce backed away as fast as his legs would take him.

"Oh, I do believe my dinner has arrived," the scorpion said, staring at Milton. The creature started forward only to have Milton somersault over his back.

"Want me? Come and get me," Milton taunted, hoping the scorpion would turn toward him and give Bruce a chance to get further away.

"Oh, yes, indeed," the scorpion said. He scuttled toward the spider, but Milton was faster and jumped to the side, out of the way of his pincers.

"You'll have to do better than that," Milton said, still baiting the creature. Milton moved further back and to the side of another rock. He heard a noise behind him and turned just in time to see another scorpion emerge from beneath that rock. This one was much larger, and she carried several babies on her back. She didn't even look at Milton but instead ran toward the first scorpion, grasping him with her pincers. Her tail lashed out over her head, trying to strike the smaller male with her poisonous barb.

While the scorpions were locked in combat, Bruce ran as fast as he could across the rest of the clearing, following Milton's lead, while Henry flew overhead, letting out little stinks as his wings beat. When they reached the far side, Bruce was so tired, he collapsed and lay panting, trying to get his breath. Henry landed and also seemed winded. The only one who was still in good shape was Milton. He stood on a mound of dirt and kept watch as the other two friends recovered from their nearly fatal encounter with the scorpions.

When Bruce felt like he could say something, he sat up. "You saved me back there, and Henry, too. Thank you again."

"You'd have done the same for me," Milton said, still scanning the area. "I don't see anything around here that could harm us, and I believe we're out of danger. You two probably need to eat something, so I'll keep watch for a while. When you've finished, you can watch while I hunt and do a little construction."

"Construction?" Henry asked.

"You'll see," Milton replied, not taking his eyes off of the area around them. He didn't want to be surprised again.

Bruce didn't see any leaves nearby that looked tender, and he wasn't in the mood to climb anywhere to do more looking. He opened his pack and pulled out the last of his apricot leaves. He broke the stem off, offered it to Henry, and began eating the leaf. He tried not to think about the scorpions and instead concentrated on enjoying the taste of the juicy leaf. Even so, he kept remembering the female with her babies and her stinger tail.

When he'd finished eating, Bruce told Milton he'd take the watch. He crawled onto the mound and began looking around. Milton bounded out a distance and began attaching his silken line to the base of shrubbery, small plants, and even grasses, running around in a circle. When he had completed one round, he moved inward and began the process over again. Each of these lines was only a little way off the ground, and each circle was attached to the one outside of it by means of other lines. After a while, Bruce could see that he was composing a web, only instead of hanging in the air, this one was suspended just a little way off the ground.

"What are you doing?" Henry asked.

"I'm spinning a web that will alert us if something comes toward us on the ground. It should vibrate enough to wake me with enough time to warn everyone to get to safety."

"Wow, that's smart!" Henry said. Milton smiled.

"Don't tell him that," Bruce said, scowling. "His head will get even fatter than it is now."

"My head is not fat. You are the one with a fat head, Bruce. Actually, it's hard to even see your head. It's like your neck just keeps going. Wait—do you even have a neck?" Milton asked, grinning. They all chuckled.

When he'd finished the web, Milton jumped beyond it and started hunting. Henry was on watch when he returned. It looked funny to see such a large mound of dirt with such a tiny bug on top of it, scouting intently for predators. Milton came inside the web circle, patting his abdomen and looking pleased with himself. Henry flew down, his wings making the soft buzzing sound they always made, and landed between his friends. They all looked very sleepy, and by the time Henry had settled into a good position, Bruce was already snoring.

Some time during the night, Milton woke, thinking Bruce's snores were getting hard to take. He turned over and tried to go back to sleep, when he heard the rumble get louder and louder. It wasn't Bruce—it was coming from beyond them in the clearing. He saw that

Henry had awakened and motioned for him to stay down and be quiet. He jumped to where Bruce was starting to rouse and put his foot over Bruce's mouth so he wouldn't make any noise.

In the moonlight, they saw a machine that looked like the ones Bruce and Milton had seen when the men worked on the road. This one was smaller, but it made the same loud noise. As they watched, the noise stopped, and a man climbed out of the machine and began walking toward them. He held a strange, purple light and a large box in one hand. In his other hand was a stick he used to poke into holes and overturn rocks. He walked along doing this for quite a while. Suddenly, he crouched down and poked the stick where a rock had been. It was hard to see what he was doing in the darkness, but when he stood up, he held a large scorpion in the air beneath his light. The creature glowed with a bright white light. The man dropped the scorpion into the box and walked back to the machine. He climbed inside and the noise started again. Then the machine moved away, back the way it had come.

Bruce had never had much contact with men until they came to work on the road by his village. They had come with big machines and had covered the dirt road with black stuff that was hot and smelled bad. When the black stuff dried, it became hard, but it didn't smell very much anymore. Bruce didn't understand why they did this, but he had heard that men often did things insects couldn't understand. His father had said it was best to stay away from them.

Bruce didn't have much love for scorpions. It's hard to feel good about something that is always trying to eat you. Still, he was upset to see this one captured and taken away.

No one said anything until the sound was gone completely. It was too dark to see each other, but the small sounds of their bodies and breathing were enough to know that they were there and settling down again.

"That was the scorpion, right? Where is the man taking her?" Henry asked.

"I don't know," Bruce said. "I've heard that men keep insects sometimes." He thought back to Sophie telling him about boys catching her in jars. "They call them 'pets.'"

"What's a pet?" Henry asked.

"Meryl, a friend of mine, told me humans keep two kinds of pets: those who want to stay with men, like Samson, a cat who chose to live with a farmer and his wife, and those who don't. The ones who don't are kept in cages."

"Do you think the scorpion will be in a cage?"

"Yes, Henry. I think so."

"Then I hope she stings him!"

Bruce couldn't help but like Henry's simple view of good and bad. "Maybe she will, Henry. Maybe she will."

Chapter 10

Carly

fter they had awakened and eaten in the morning, they moved out again. Staying under the trees wouldn't keep them safe from scorpions or large spiders lurking under rocks, or lizards and frogs hiding in the bushes, but it helped avoid overhead predators. Milton did his best to keep watch as they moved through the patches of grass and leaves.

They came to the spot where the man had captured the scorpion during the night. They saw the large ruts where the machine had stood in the soft, muddy ground, and the area smelled of strange odors. Milton jumped onto a tree stump where he could get a better view, and Henry flew over the spot, landing safely on the other side. When Bruce was nearly past the scene, he felt something sharp poke him in the side. As he looked down, it happened again, and he saw a tiny scorpion flicking her tail over her back and stabbing her stinger into his side. He stepped away as he flipped the baby onto her back.

"That isn't very nice!" Bruce said to the creature who was struggling to turn herself over.

"I want to eat you," she said. "You look tasty." She wiggled this way and that, but only succeeded in digging a hole beneath her.

"I certainly do not look tasty," Bruce said, wondering how a creature as small as she was could possibly think about eating a caterpillar. "Besides, I'm too big for you to eat."

"No you're not," she said, righting herself. She rushed at him again, flicking her stinger over her head. Bruce grabbed her by her tail, careful to avoid the stinger, and held her in the air, very much like the man had done with the other scorpion. The little creature wiggled and squirmed.

She was nearly transparent, with just a hint of the brown that would come later. She looked like a tiny copy of the scorpion the man had taken during the night. Bruce worried that he might get sick from the poke she had given him earlier, but so far he felt fine.

"Put me down!" she said, and when Bruce didn't react, she tried to grab his legs with her front claws.

"Settle down and act properly, or I will hold you here forever," Bruce said, knowing this wasn't true, but he couldn't think of what else to say to the creature.

"You'd better do what he says, because if you don't, I'll spin you in my spider silk," Milton added.

After a while, she grew tired of kicking her legs and trying to grab at Bruce, and she hung quietly.

"If I put you down, will you be nice and not poke me again?"

She narrowed her eyes, puckered her mouth, and sighed. "Okay. I guess I'll have to eat someone else."

Bruce had to work hard not to smile. He put the scorpion on the ground again, as far away from himself as he could reach. He took a defensive posture in case she decided not to keep her word.

Carly

She stood quietly, looking at Milton and Bruce.

"Where's your mother?" Bruce asked, but as he said it, he realized she was probably the scorpion who had been captured by the man.

"She was holding us on her back, the way she always did, and then she went way high up, and I fell off." In his mind, Bruce could see the man holding the glowing scorpion under his light. "She never came back."

"Are there other scorpions around here who could take care of you?" Milton asked.

"No, I can't go near them. Mama said they would eat us. She even said we would have to leave her and go off on our own when we got bigger, because she would want to eat us, too."

"That's right," Milton said. "That happens with some spiders, too."

"You poked me with your stinger," Bruce said, "but I don't feel any poison. I don't think you're ready to be on your own yet."

"Mama said our poison would come later. I thought maybe I was old enough to hunt now. I'll just have to stay out of the way until I get bigger."

"We could bring her with us!" Henry said, buzzing above them in a circle. "We won't eat her, and we can keep her safe until she's big enough to catch her own food."

Bruce frowned, but Milton spoke quickly. "She could ride on your back, Bruce," he said with a grin.

"After she tried to eat me?" Bruce said, looking down at the little scorpion with a sour face. Then he thought about leaving her out here alone while she was so very small, and he knew he couldn't do that, either.

63

"You can ride on my back," he said, sighing again. "But don't even think about poking me. If you do, I'll leave you behind and never look back," he said, trying to sound fierce.

The scorpion pouted. "I won't poke you or try to eat you again. I really shouldn't need to eat for a while. Mama said we could survive for a long, long time without eating, if we had to, and I'm really not that hungry—you just looked tasty. "

Bruce scowled. "I do not look tasty. Stop that."

Milton did a somersault and landed next to Bruce, startling him again. "She's right," he said, grinning. "You do look tasty. It's all in your point of view."

Bruce gave Milton a dirty look and turned back to the scorpion. "What's your name?"

"I don't have a name yet. We don't get names until we go out on our own."

"Hmmm. Like it or not, you're on your own now," Bruce said.

"We could call her Carly," Henry said, landing on a rock so that he and the scorpion were nearly eye to eye. "Carly is my sister's name, and she was always getting into trouble. I think that's a good name."

"Pleased to meet you, Carly," Milton said, and the little scorpion smiled. She crawled onto Bruce's back and hung onto his skin. "You don't have as many places to hold onto as my mama did, but you are soft."

"Well, hang on, Carly. We have a long way to go yet." As Bruce began walking, he wondered again at the strange things that happened when he was away from home. He had a baby scorpion riding on his back! He shook his head and kept walking.

Chapter 11

To the Shore

By midday, they reached the shore. It was very busy. Besides being a place where boats were tied to large, wooden structures, small groups of people were everywhere, eating and walking about, and there were open areas where other people hung poles in the water and pulled out fish. On one side of the wooden docks was a large grassy area where people sat and children played together.

Near the boats, men went here and there, picking things up and putting them down and then carrying more things. Bruce knew the men were loading and unloading the boats because Milton had told him about this when they first met.

There were so many boats! Bruce wondered how they could possibly learn which one was going to the island. Perhaps all the boats went there?

"Look," Milton said, jumping up and down. "It's the boat that brought me here! I know because it's green and white and its bell is missing—that broke while we came over. I know it's the same one!"

"Do you think it would go back where you came from?" Bruce asked.

"I hope so," Milton said, but then he lost a little of his excitement. "Except we need to go to the island,

and we don't know if that's the same place." He looked back at the boat, his expression a little sad, but then he brightened again. "Still, it could be. That would be great."

They moved down the ramp to the dock, being careful to stay out of the way so the people moving back and forth didn't step on Bruce or Milton. Overhead, out of the way of the men and the hustle and bustle, Henry flew from pole to pole, being careful to avoid the seabirds who owned most of the territory around here. Bruce crawled in the spaces between the planks of the dock, while Milton stayed above, jumping this way and that, avoiding the feet and crates of goods that moved quickly by them. Carly moved around as necessary to be on "top" of Bruce, no matter which way he was facing. From time to time, Milton would rejoin Bruce and tell him what was going on above.

"We're almost to the first boat. It's not as large as some of the others. It's painted blue and white, and there are many people and machines on it. I don't see any boxes on this boat, not like some of the others. Just many people and machines."

Bruce and Carly emerged at the end of the planks and looked down at the water below. The ocean was a deep blue-green, and it lapped against the posts and piers below the dock and against the hulls of the boats in the water. It was a nice sound, but Bruce instinctively knew better than to get too close to the water—it was unpredictable and never stopped moving. He'd almost drowned in a water trough once, so he knew he'd never survive if he fell in here.

He was eager to find the right boat and get settled.

He looked around, hoping they might meet a creature who could give them more information.

He heard something and stopped to listen. He thought it was a bird scolding and another screeching in reply. He'd never heard sounds like that, although it reminded him of the noises Samson the cat had made when he was angry.

"Milton, do you hear those cries? I think we should head that way. Maybe one of those animals will be friendly and can help us decide which boat to take."

"A good plan. Nothing to lose, as long as we're careful not to come out of hiding until we're sure it's safe."

"I'll fly ahead and look," Henry said. He'd been resting on top of a pillar where he had a good view of the dock and the creatures on it. "I see a lot of activity going on further down the dock. I'll be right back."

"Be careful!" Milton and Bruce said together. Henry was younger than they were, and it seemed that they were taking care of him as much as they were now caring for Carly.

"Don't fly too high—the seabirds will catch you," Milton said.

"And stay out of heavy wind," Bruce added. "Carly, how are you doing?"

"I'm sleepy," she said. She walked up on top of Bruce's head and leaned over until she was looking him in the eyes. "Are we going to stop soon? I want a nap."

"No, Carly. We're going on until we find the right boat. Then we can stop and rest."

"O-kay," the scorpion said, obviously unhappy

she was not getting her way. "Can I ride on him for a while?" she said, pointing to Milton.

Bruce looked over at his friend, who seemed to have little choice but to say yes. Milton jumped over next to Bruce, and Carly climbed onto his back. She giggled. "Your hairs tickle!"

"I'm glad you find me amusing," Milton said, making a sour face.

"I find you amusing, too," Bruce said with a smirk. "Let's go—I want to find this boat before I'm too old to care anymore." He set off down the planks and Milton followed, taking care not to jump and lose Carly.

They had traveled quite far when Henry returned. "It's horrible!" he said, out of breath and flying in circles above them. "They're in cages, and they can't get free!"

"Henry, slow down," Bruce said, as the little bug landed in front of him on the wooden planks. Bruce could tell that Henry had let out a stink recently. "Catch your breath, and tell me what you're talking about."

Henry breathed in and out several times, and the redness in his face cleared a little. "The animals. There are lots of animals further down the dock. They say they were caught or raised by men and put in cages. They are being taken to the island. The boat down there is going to the island, but they said you shouldn't get on it because no animal on the boat is safe. I don't know the different kinds of animals, and there are many sizes, but they're all so sad!"

It was too bad about the animals, but Bruce was excited to hear that Henry had found the boat going to the island. He felt a renewed sense of energy now that they were closer to his goal. "Lead the way. I don't know if there is anything we can do for the animals, but we'll see after we get there." Bruce thought back to all that he and Milton had gone through in the bat cave and wondered how they always seemed to find themselves in these situations.

Bruce hurried down the planks, and when he passed one more boat, he saw row after row of cages lined up on the docks. Men were carrying the cages up a long ramp onto the boat. Other boxes were being lifted into the air by machines. Bruce didn't want to go anywhere near those. His father had told him about machines that could crush him or suck him in. They would have to find a way to get onto the boat without going near the ramp, too, as many men were walking back and forth there.

They moved toward the cages. Bruce saw creatures he'd never seen before. Some had very long fur; others had short fur but long claws. There were snakes and large birds with beautiful, colored feathers. Bruce had never seen so many different animals together. He wondered why the men were moving them to the island.

The snake spotted Milton and called out, "Spider! Please! Open the latch on this cage and set me free!"

Milton looked around to see if any men were coming. Seeing no one, he let Carly climb down and jumped up on the latch of the cage. He tried to push it to one side, but it wouldn't move. He tried pushing the other way, but it was stuck. Milton called Bruce to come and help. Once Bruce had crawled up, they tried pushing the latch together, but they couldn't budge it.

"I'm sorry, snake. We can't open the latch," Bruce said, crawling down from the cage. Milton jumped down and landed next to Bruce. He extended his leg down to Carly who climbed up again.

The snake looked sad and lay on the bottom of his cage. "Thank you for trying," he said, gazing off into the distance.

Bruce felt anger such as he hadn't felt in a long time. He remembered feeling the same way when Julia told him about the bats being held prisoner in the cave. He couldn't understand how someone, anyone, would want to hurt or imprison someone else. It was happening all over again. But what could he—they—do?

Bruce turned and found himself nearly eye to eye with a snail. Snails were common near Bruce's home, and he wasn't alarmed. This one was smaller and his shell was more brightly colored than those he'd seen before. The snail poked his eyestalks toward Bruce.

"Oh, excuse me," the snail said, squinting. "Didn't see you coming. Now aren't you the different one! I've never seen anything like you before. What are you exactly?" The snail poked his eyestalks further forward until his eyes were almost on top of Bruce.

"I'm a caterpillar. I'll turn into a butter—" Bruce started to say, but then stopped short, realizing he didn't know what he'd become.

"Butter, you say? I once had some butter when a sailor's lunch fell overboard. Quite a feast, that was! Well, you learn something new every day, I always say. I'll have to tell Jonas about you. Jonas is always telling me things. Now I'll have something I can share with him, and I'm sure he never knew that caterpillars turn into butter. Fancy that!"

"No, I didn't mean—"

"And you, my hairy friend," the snail said, addressing Milton and turning one eyestalk his way. "Who are you? Did you come with him?"

"Yes, I did. I'm a jumping spider, and my name is—"

"A jumping spider! Oh my goodness. I once met a flea who said she was with a circus. Now she could jump! Are you a performer, too?"

"Um, no, I jump because—"

"Well, if you ever need work, you might find her and ask if they need anyone else to join them. That is, unless you eat fleas. You don't eat fleas, do you?"

"Uh, no, not usually. I prefer to eat—"

"Well, that should work out well, then. See, it's settled. I love it when I can help those in need. And Jonas tells me I talk too much. If I didn't talk this much, I'd never have found out that you wanted to be in the circus, or that caterpillars turn into butter, now would I? Well, my fine fellows, I'll be going unless there is something else I can do for you. You don't need my help anymore, do you?" He started to move forward, bumped into Bruce, and his eyestalks retracted into his head.

"Oh, excuse me. I didn't see you there. May I help you?"

"Actually, we would appreciate it if you could tell us if this is the boat that goes to the island," Bruce said.

The snail's eyestalks slowly extended, and he squinted at Bruce again. "My, my. It's uncanny! You look just like a caterpillar I met only a little while ago. Never did tell me his name or what he wanted, although I did learn an interesting fact I'm going to share with Jonas, a friend of mine. Well, if you must know, I learned that caterpillars are where butter comes from. You see, after a while in the hot sun, they simply melt, and there you have it! Yes, I never would have guessed that, either, but it's what he said. Well, if you don't need my help, I'll be going now. Goodbye."

Bruce stepped aside to let the snail pass, which took quite a while. When he had gone, there was a slimy trail where he'd been. Bruce started to hop over it, when a seabird flew close overhead, its shadow hiding the sun and scaring him. Bruce's leap went wrong, and he fell on his side in the slime. The bird continued on its way, and Bruce got to his feet, feeling relieved that the bird hadn't noticed them, but his side was gooey, covered in the clear substance that was both sticky and slippery at the same time.

He didn't have time to do anything about it. Looking up, Bruce saw a man coming toward the cages. He motioned for Milton and Carly to crouch down. Bruce scrambled into a crack between the planks, while Milton grabbed Carly and hid behind a crate. Bruce hoped the man wouldn't notice Henry, who stood motionless on a rope leading from one of the boats to the dock.

Bruce suddenly had an idea about how they could gain access to the island boat without being stepped on. This boat also had ropes securing it to the dock. All they had to do was climb one of the ropes and they would be on board without having to come near a human. Having figured out this plan, Bruce felt some of his anxiety disappear, but he still felt a stab of regret at having to leave the animals locked in their cages.

The man piled the cage containing the snake on top of another cage, this one holding a furry creature Bruce didn't recognize. The furry creature hissed and spit at the snake, and it was obvious that they were enemies. Perhaps the snake normally ate creatures like the furry one, or perhaps the other way around? Then the man picked up both cages and walked away with them, up the ramp and into the boat. Bruce signaled to Milton that it was all right to come out.

"We can crawl up that rope over there," he said, pointing to a line at the front of the boat. "No one should bother us going that way, and we'll be on the boat before long."

"Good idea! Let's go."

Bruce motioned in the direction where they were headed. Henry nodded, and Bruce and Milton set off. Carly rode behind Milton's head, bobbing up and down as he walked along.

A large, white bird flew overhead, and then several more followed. The travelers stopped moving until the birds were well past. Bruce had never seen birds like these before. Some were as large as hawks, and a few were simply enormous. These great birds would dive into the water and come up with great numbers of fish in their mouths, swallowing them whole. The smaller birds were also frightening because they liked to fight with one another, biting and snapping in the air. They were unruly and loud, and Bruce didn't like them. They were nothing like the birds he was used to seeing at home.

That thought made him sigh again. They had come so far, but they were no closer to finding anything than when they set out. He wished . . . no, he'd learned that wishing didn't get anything done. He pushed the thoughts from his mind and continued walking past the rest of the cages. Many of the animals asked if Bruce or Milton could free them. Others simply slept or didn't open their eyes. Bruce wondered how he would feel if he'd been caught in a cage and held prisoner. When he'd been caught by Stang and held in the small room of the cave, he had assumed he would get free somehow, and he never felt completely trapped. Perhaps these creatures felt that way now. No, he thought, it looked like most of them had given up the idea that they would ever be free again. It made Bruce very sad.

They reached the rope leading to the boat and began climbing. A number of times on this journey, Bruce thought it would have been better if he had simply changed into whatever it was he would become. Then he wouldn't be here, climbing around and trying to avoid predators, or, if he were, he would have been able to fly, and it wouldn't have taken so long to get anywhere. Milton could jump far and was very quick; Henry could fly, at least for short distances. Even little Carly was faster than Bruce, who was the slow one on this journey. Without someone like Meryl to help get him from place to place, he realized now just how slow he really was. His friends hadn't complained, but he believed they were probably tired of waiting for him to catch up.

These thoughts vanished when Bruce reached the top of the rope and looked down into the boat. It was huge, with wood and metal and ropes and men everywhere. Some of the men were getting on the boat, walking with crates and cages in their arms, and handing these off to other men who took them down inside where they disappeared. Other crates were being lowered onto the boat by machines. It was a bustle of activity, and Bruce wondered where they should go in order to remain out of the way.

Milton poked him, pointing toward an opening in a wooden structure not far from where they stood. Bruce climbed closer and, looking inside, he saw trees and bushes and realized why Milton thought this would be a good place. They did look appetizing, and Bruce realized how hungry he was again. He never seemed to get enough to eat when they were on journeys like this.

They crawled up to the opening and Bruce wondered why this small forest was on the boat. One of the branches touched the opening and Bruce crawled onto it. It felt funny—not like any branch he'd felt before. He walked a little further and decided to sample one of the leaves. He took a bite, or tried to. The leaf wouldn't tear, and he couldn't pull it apart or chew it. These were odd plants—plants you couldn't eat! Well, at least it was a safe place to hide, Bruce thought, but his visions of easy food during the trip disappeared.

Carly climbed down from Milton's back and settled onto a group of leaves that formed a snug little bed. The others rested, too, looking out of the opening to the sky and the docks. They watched as the rest of the animal crates and cages were loaded on board. A little while after the last of those was brought up, Bruce felt a rumbling, a rattling through the boards and metal of the boat. Then he saw men releasing the ropes that tied it to the dock and watched as the boat moved away. The boat was moving. They were on their way!

Chapter 12

On Board the Boat

During the first day of their journey on the boat, Bruce and his companions rested in the small compartment that housed the inedible plants. Bruce couldn't understand what kind of plants these were that had no sap for Henry to drink and no edible leaves for him to eat. After exploring a bit, Henry reported that all the stems and leaves were the same. Bruce opened his pack and pulled out an apple leaf for them to share.

Milton left to go exploring, saying he was hungry, too. It wasn't long before he returned and told them what he'd seen. "I went as far as I could, jumping from one place to another and staying out of the way of the men. They're everywhere. They walk around and sit or lie down wherever they please. Oh—there's also a cat. It doesn't look anything like Samson—it's gray and black with stripes and quite thin—but it caught a mouse while I was watching, so we have to be careful. I did find a wonderful area where a man prepares meals. This room has flies and other insects and also some leafy greens that you two might like to eat. If you run out of food in your pack, we can make our way back there and see what might be tasty."

The next day, Milton ventured out again while

Bruce, Henry, and Carly remained behind. After a while, though, the three grew tired of sitting while Milton explored. Bruce crawled out of the opening and looked around. He wouldn't go far—just enough to see a little more of the boat and find out what was going on firsthand.

He inched his way out the opening and up one of the boards, until he was sitting on top of the wooden structure. He had a view of the deck from here, and he saw that Milton was right: men were everywhere, moving about, talking to one another. Beyond the boat, the ocean seemed to go on forever with nothing in sight except clouds in the sky. Most of those were white and puffy, but on one side they were gray and dark. Bruce wondered if another storm was coming.

He also wondered where the animals in the cages were kept on the boat. He wished he'd been able to help the snake and the others to get free, and he wondered if he could do something for them, now that he had time to think and figure it out. Milton hadn't mentioned seeing any cages. He'd have to ask him about that when he returned.

The air outside was nice after being cooped up in the small room. Bruce liked the feel of the sun on his skin and the breeze that tickled his feelers. Bruce could hear waves slapping the sides of the boat. He was surprised to see many sleek creatures in the water that he'd never seen before. They were gray and white and very large, although much smaller than the boat, and they swam in groups, jumping in and out of the water and making loud noises.

Bruce heard some sounds behind him and turned

to see Carly and Henry climbing up from the opening. They came and sat next to him, also looking out to sea.

"You're both too small to be out here," Bruce said, moving around to shield them from the wind so they wouldn't be blown away.

Henry's eyes were huge. "It's so big," he said. "The ocean is even bigger now than when we got on the boat."

It seemed that way to Bruce, too. Because they couldn't see anything except water around them, the ocean did seem bigger, and he felt even smaller than he usually did.

He gathered the others close and curled around them for protection. They sat back against the wall. After a time, he began to feel sleepy. He knew they shouldn't stay out in the open when he was getting tired. But the sun felt so good, he decided it would be all right to stay just a little longer.

The next thing he knew, Henry was buzzing in his face. Bruce sat up with a start. He'd fallen asleep. There was a terrible smell again—Henry's stink—and he realized Henry was yelling at him.

"Get down! Hide!"

Bruce scrambled to his feet, taking care to shield the small bug and scorpion. As he did, he saw the ship's cat heading for the patch of sunshine they were enjoying.

Bruce knew they would never make it back to the opening of the plant room without the cat seeing them. He motioned for the others to move around behind the wooden structure, and he followed. He wasn't sure if they should stay outside, but he didn't see anywhere else they could go.

As they huddled there, a shadow fell over the area that had been sunny moments before. Looking up, Bruce saw that the dark clouds had moved closer, and one of them was blocking the sun. He heard the raindrops landing around him before he felt them.

"We have to move inside before the storm gets worse. Come on—I'm going to carry you."

Carly climbed onto Bruce's back and settled behind his head, followed by Henry who sat in the curl of her tail. When he was sure both of them were holding on tightly, Bruce darted away from the box. Just before starting down to the opening, he looked back and saw the cat batting at something small and black, trying to catch it. Then he realized that the small, black thing was Milton!

With the cat distracted, he told Carly to take Henry back inside the plant room and wait for him to come back. As Carly started down, Henry rose into the air and flew toward Milton and the cat.

"Henry! Come back! What are you doing?" Bruce cried.

Henry continued flying through the raindrops until Bruce couldn't see him anymore.

Bruce was beside himself. He tried to think what he could do to save Milton from the cat without being eaten himself. As he watched, however, he realized Milton was actually jumping around and over the cat. He was taunting it, and Bruce understood that Milton had done this to give him and the others time to get away. He knew that Milton wouldn't stop his game with the cat until he knew his friends were safe, so Bruce crawled after Carly and made his way inside the window. He thought Milton might be able to avoid the cat's sharp claws, but what about Henry?

Bruce and Carly waited and waited, hoping Milton and Henry would be along any moment. Bruce knew the spider had taken a huge risk. Still no Milton. No Henry. The rain was stronger now, and the sound of the drops hitting the boat was all that they could hear. Bruce's heart ached. He was beginning to believe that his friends might be lost. He knew why Milton had taunted the cat, but what was Henry thinking? All of this was happening because of his stupid wish to know about his egg parents and to find out whether he was a butterfly or a moth. He knew Milton wanted to see his family again, but the real reason Milton had come with Bruce was to help him with his quest. He'd been so selfish, and now maybe . . .

He felt the tears building and squeezed his eyes shut. He mustn't cry—he didn't want Carly to see that.

"Henry told me that Milton fought bats and that he's very brave. Henry is a tough little bug, and he can take care of himself better than you think, just like I can," Carly said. "Besides, Mama said we shouldn't think of bad things unless they happen, and then only to figure out what to do. Milton and Henry will come back."

Bruce opened his eyes and looked at the scorpion. Carly didn't seem so small anymore—she was starting to get her brown coloring, and she did appear larger. He swallowed, regaining his composure. "Your mama was wise."

"I thought so," Carly said, smiling.

"Okay, then. We'll think good thoughts. Milton

81

and Henry will be here soon."

"How about now?" Milton said, as he sailed through the opening and landed next to Bruce. Henry was hanging on tightly to the fur behind Milton's head. When the spider stopped, Henry let go and somersaulted into the leaves, which cushioned his fall.

"Whee!" Henry squealed, as he righted himself and stood looking at his friends. "That was exciting!"

"You scared us!" Bruce said, feeling angry and glad at the same time. "What were you two thinking?"

"Well, I was coming back, when I saw the cat heading this way. I spotted you asleep outside, and I worried that the cat would find you. I decided to get his attention. That's when Henry spotted us and woke you. I think I could have stayed away from the cat, but it was Henry's stinkiness that saved the day." Milton raised one foreleg in a salute to the tiny bug. "He came up behind the cat and sprayed his odor right into the cat's face. You should have heard him howl! He backed off and ran in the other direction. Henry's a pretty tough little bug!"

Bruce was still scowling a little, having been worried that he'd lost his friends, but his joy at having everyone together again overcame his upset, and he realized he was hungry again. He opened his pack, pulled out two leaves, bit off the stems and gave them to Henry. As he began chewing, Milton said he'd eaten some mealworms that he found feeding on a sack of spilled grain. He promised to bring some of them back for Carly the next day. He said he'd found where the animals were still locked in their cages—a small room not far from where they were now. He then described another near-miss with the cat, and Bruce became worried again, only to look over at Carly who squinted at him. She climbed up the leaves until she was sitting next to Milton. The spider wrapped his foreleg around her, and she looked happy.

The rain began coming down more heavily then, and occasional gusts of wind blew water in through the opening where it landed on the leaves of the plants. Bruce took that opportunity to drink from the drops, but when the wind grew too strong, he moved further behind the leaves that kept him drier.

Bruce was glad to have these friends with him, each one protecting the other as best they could. He settled down to try and sleep as the storm blew outside.

Chapter 13

The Storm

Bruce awoke when his head hit a branch on the tree in which he slept. It was dark, but flashes of lightning illuminated the interior of their space, and he could see that all the travelers were awake. Bruce crept along the branch until he got to the opening where he could see what was happening outside. Milton followed and stood next to him.

The boat rolled and turned as waves slapped its sides and water crashed over the deck. The rain slashed through the air and made it hard for him to see out the opening, even when the lightning lit the sky. Suddenly, a large zigzag of light illuminated everything, and the clap of thunder that followed was a huge, booming sound. Their space was quickly awash in a horrid stink. Bruce held his breath, trying not to take in the terrible smell, and he kept his eyes shut to stop the burning. When he opened them again, he saw that Henry had covered his ears and was trembling.

"Henry, there's no need to be afraid. The sound won't hurt you."

"My mom always told me that, but it still makes me jump."

"As long as you stay inside, the lightning can't hurt you, and thunder is only a sound that follows the lightning. We're safe here," Bruce said.

No sooner had he said this than the sky became a dazzling white. The wood planks above their heads split with a crash, and splinters of wood flew past. There was a strong, strange smell in the air, followed by smoke. Those smells were soon joined with another horrid smell from Henry.

Bruce winced as he felt rain pelting down on him and he squinted upward. The planks above their heads were broken, leaving an opening where the rain was falling in. Then he saw the fire! The boards above them were burning, even as the rain fell, sizzling as it tried to put out the fire. When Bruce heard men crying out close to them, he knew they must get away.

"Milton, we've got to get everyone out of here! Do you know another place that would be safe?"

"Follow me!" Milton said, moving toward the opening.

"Out there?" Bruce asked. "I think we should stay inside!"

"If we do, we'll be crushed when the men start running around, and it sounds like they're doing just that. Our best bet is to go out, crawl along the ledge, and down into another room like this one."

Bruce frowned and looked again at the fire and the rain, as lightning again lit the sky, and the thunder that followed was as loud as before. "All right. I'm coming."

He moved quickly to the opening. As he poked his head through, he felt the stinging rain, and the wind threatened to blow him away. "Milton, I don't think I can hang onto the wood in this wind, and I'm sure

Henry and Carly will be blown away. Is there another way to go and stay inside?"

Milton thought for a moment. "The area where the animals are in their cages isn't too far, and we can get there without going out. We'll have to stay out of the way of the men, though."

"That sounds better. Henry—Carly—are you okay?"

Henry was still trembling, but he took a deep breath and said, "I'm okay. I'm fine. Don't worry about me." He paused. "I'm sorry about the stink."

"Not as sorry as I am," Carly said, as she climbed up Milton's leg and sat behind his head.

"Come on, then."

The small room was filling with smoke, and the travelers began to cough. Milton led the way down to the floor. He moved past the rows of inedible trees to a door that Bruce hadn't seen. They squeezed through a crack beneath that door.

They were now in a dark hallway. Since Henry saw better in the dark than the rest of them, he led the way. Milton told him to keep going until they came to another door. Then he tied a silken line from Henry to Bruce and then to himself so that they could stay together. Bruce wasn't entirely sure that this was a good arrangement, as he would get the brunt of any odor if Henry became excited, but he didn't see a better way.

Reaching the end of the hallway, they came to another door and crawled under it into a large room. There was a light on one of the walls, and Bruce saw cages piled all around and on top of one another. The room smelled of the animals—mostly fur, but also other smells that weren't as nice as fur. Bruce's instinctive reaction was to back away, since most furry animals seemed to find eating caterpillars was a treat. He knew these animals were in cages, though, and he made himself keep up with Henry, who was doing well in the lead, considering how scared he was. Bruce hoped Henry would continue being calm. Once they'd reached their destination, Bruce chewed through the strand of silk that bound him to the others.

"What's going on? Is someone there?" called a voice from one of the cages in the back of the room. The voice was high-pitched, and the animal talked very fast.

"A caterpillar, a spider, a scorpion, and a bug," Bruce said, carefully leaving out the "stink" part of Henry's description. "There's a storm outside with lightning and thunder."

"Oh," the voice said with a sniff. "I hoped you were larger, like a cat, maybe, or even a rat. I don't think you'll be much help in setting us free."

Bruce bristled, since they had been dismissed as "no help" without the animal even knowing them. Yet what the creature said was true. He didn't know how to set them free. The cages were too hard to open.

"No help at all, by the look of them," said a furry creature in one of the cages in front. When the animal spoke, Bruce saw that he had large, white teeth. His fur was brown, and he had short legs with tiny feet and toes. His body was skinny and ended in a long tail. The creature stood and put his front feet on the bars of his cage.

"I don't see you doing much to help us, Eugene," said a female from the next cage. She looked like

Eugene, except she was light brown and tan.

"Well, I can't reach your cage latch, or I'd have you out of there in no time," Eugene said.

Bruce looked around. "I think we'll be safe in here."

"Didn't you say that in the last room?" Carly said, rolling her eyes.

Milton did a somersault, catapulting Carly off his back. She landed in the straw that covered much of the floor. When she got back to her feet, she gave Milton a dirty look. He made a face back at her.

"Yes, I did," Bruce said. "If you have a better idea, Carly, share it with the rest of us. Meanwhile, let's find a place to settle down that's out of the way. Maybe over there?" He pointed to a space under a low shelf that stuck out from the wall.

"Hey, look over here," Henry said from a corner behind the cages. "There's lots of food for everybody. Well, maybe not for you, Carly. What do you eat, anyway?"

"Nice of you to ask," Carly said, turning toward the sound of Henry's voice. "But I don't. At least, not on this trip. I still wish I'd had Bruce for my first meal. But he's decided not to cooperate, so I'll go hungry for a while. If I see something that looks appetizing, I'll let you know."

"I'm sure you will," muttered Bruce, wondering for a moment why they'd brought Carly along. It seemed like she could take care of herself very well without their help.

"That spot you picked out is fine," Milton said, and he leaped over to it in a single jump. Bruce headed that way, looking into the cage on his left, where the furry animal was watching him. He'd gone a short way when a slimy body emerged out of the straw in front of him. Bruce was startled and he reared up, holding out his claws, only to realize it was the snail he'd met on the dock earlier.

"Oh, it's you," Bruce said, relieved, as he lowered himself onto the straw. The snail poked his eyestalks closer to Bruce.

"No, no, no, it's you," the snail said, making his way out of the straw. "Aren't you the same caterpillar I met before? Let's see. Where was that again? No, wait, I remember. You were the one joining the circus with the fleas, weren't you ... or was that your friend? Everyone I meet tells me so many things about themselves that it's hard for me to keep track of the facts. Well, tell me—how can I help you today?"

Bruce felt exasperated. The snail was rude—never listening to anyone and always talking. Still, there was something humorous about him, too, so it was hard to be bothered by him. Bruce started to reply, when he heard in his mind the last thing the snail had said: "How can I help you today?" He looked at his side, where the snail's sticky goo still clung to his skin.

"You *can* help me," Bruce said.

"Wonderful," the snail replied, even as one of his eyestalks turned to look at Milton while the other stayed fixed on Bruce. "I love being of service to my fellow snails. No, wait, you're not snails, are you? I don't know what you are, do I? Ah, well, it doesn't matter. 'A friend in need,' and all that, I always say. Now, get on with it. Don't dilly dally. I don't have all day, and I'm not as young as I used to be."

"Would you give us some of your . . . your slime?"

"Ewwww!" Carly said, closing her eyes and scrunching up her face.

"Certainly," the snail said, turning both eyestalks toward Bruce. "But why?"

"I want to free these animals from their cages. I'm not sure if it will work, but your slime might make the locks slippery enough that we can slide the latches open."

"That's a great plan!" Milton said. He somersaulted and landed next to Bruce, startling the snail, who pulled in his eyestalks. A long time passed before he let them out again, one at a time. Bruce wondered if they would have to go through introductions again. He pushed his way in front of Milton so the snail could see him instead.

"There you are again. You disappeared for a while. That happens a lot. In any case, you want some of my slime, you say? We snails don't call it slime, you know. We call it 'slick.' Slime is such a . . . well, such a slimy word, isn't it? But I'm happy to help you, especially since you'll be going away to join the circus soon. It's the very least I can do. Are these animals going with you?"

"Yes, of course," Bruce said, not wanting to make the conversation longer. "That's why you have to help me set them free, so we can all go together."

"Oh, wonderful! I feel giddy! I will have to tell Jonas that I helped to make the circus a reality, all with my slick. Who would have thought it?"

"So, please, Mr. Snail—how do we go about gathering your 'slick'?"

"Please, my name is Sebastian, and it might be easier if I crawl up the cages and leave the slick on the locks myself. That would work, wouldn't it?"

Bruce thought it might, and it would be easier than trying to collect the fluid. Milton nodded, bouncing up and down.

"Great suggestion, Sebastian. I'm pleased to meet you. I'm Bruce, and this is Milton, Henry, and Car—hey, where is Carly?"

"Shh. I'm trying to sneak up on my dinner," Carly whispered from far behind the animal cages.

Bruce decided not to worry about her for the moment and turned back to the snail. "Sebastian, would you crawl up this cage," he said, moving toward the container that held the furry female animal next to Eugene, "and leave some of your slick on the lock? Then we'll try to open it."

"Certainly, yes, of course."

Sebastian began the slow process of moving across the straw, then up the corner of the cage where the metal was solid, and then across the front. When he reached the lock, he stopped, wiggled his tail, and began moving across the mechanism, leaving a thick layer of goo on the sliding latch. Bruce didn't care what Sebastian called it—it was slime, plain and simple, and he couldn't wait to get the stuff off of him. After crawling all over the lock, Sebastian began the slow process of turning around and retracing his path.

As Sebastian came down one side of the cage, Bruce climbed up the other. When he reached the latch, Milton jumped up, landing right next to him, chuckling to himself as Bruce fumed.

"One of these days, I'm going to get you," he said, but his smile revealed that he enjoyed this game as much as Milton.

Bruce looked through the bars at the furry animal. "We need a promise from you before we go further. My friends and I have an agreement, and we need you to agree to the same thing before we set you free. You must promise not to eat any of us or each other while we're on this ship. You must either go hungry or find other things to eat until we get where we're going."

"The men come and feed us twice each day," the furry creature said, "so we don't need to eat you or each other. I promise."

"Do the rest of you promise, too?"

There were murmurs of "yes, sure, set us free!" and similar replies.

"Okay. Let's see if we can do this."

Bruce and Milton pushed and pulled, but the latch wouldn't move. They tried and tried, but the slime hadn't made any difference. They still couldn't open it.

"Thanks for trying to free us," the furry creature said. "You're brave and smart, and I hoped your idea might work."

"Let me try," Carly said from below the cage. "My dinner wouldn't cooperate any more than you did. I might as well see what I can do to help you."

Bruce's eyes narrowed as he stared at the little scorpion. "I don't see what you could do that Milton and I can't, but you're welcome to try."

Carly crawled up the cage and quickly reached the latch. She was growing very fast. Her color was almost entirely brown now, and she had nearly doubled her size. She turned so that her backside was toward the latch. Then she uncurled her tail, slid her stinger under the latch, and flicked it upward. "Maybe if we all work together?" she said.

Neither Bruce nor Milton had realized that the latch had to lift before it would slide. Bruce's glare faded to a grin. "Carly, you're brilliant! Lift the latch again, and Milton and I will push it open."

"No problem," Carly said. When the others were ready, she flicked the latch up with her tail, and Bruce and Milton put all their might into pushing it sideways. Without the pressure of the latch being down, it slid easily, and both of them went flying as the cage door swung open. Milton was used to somersaulting in the air, and he landed expertly on the straw. Bruce tumbled and turned a few times, eventually rolling in the straw not far from Milton. He stood and shook his body, trying to get rid of the dust and bits of straw that stuck to him, especially where the goo still clung to his side.

The furry creature leaped out of the cage and stretched, reaching out with each front leg and then those in back. "Oh, that feels wonderful!" she said, arching her back. "I've been in that cage for so long, I thought my back might have a permanent curl." She turned to look at the travelers. "I owe you a debt of gratitude, my small ones. I heard your names when you introduced yourself to this kindly snail," she said, putting her nose next to Sebastian and sniffing him, causing him to retract his eyestalks and pull his head away. "I am Lilly," she said, dipping her head down toward the travelers. Leaning her head toward the animal in the next cage, she said, "That's Eugene.

We were raised in the same place, and humans were always good to us, until this trip. Here, they're mean, and they spray us with water when we make too much noise."

"They don't give us enough food, either," Eugene said, looking longingly at the sacks of food stacked against the wall. "Can you get me out of my cage, too? I'd love to see if some of those sacks have good things to eat."

"Oh, and me! Set me free!" said the high-pitched voice that had spoken before.

"And me, too!" said another, and soon the room was filled with loud calls from the rest of the animals to have their cages opened.

Lilly let out a shrill bark. The room quieted, but then the creatures began wrinkling their noses and moaning.

"Oh, Henry!" Bruce said, closing his eyes against the acrid fumes. "We have to work on that!"

"Sorry," Henry said, flapping his small wings, trying to disperse the smell a bit. "I didn't expect her to make that loud noise."

"For someone so small," Lilly said, "you pack a wallop! I'm sorry I scared you." Then she jumped on top of her cage so that the rest of the animals could see her. "All of you—keep quiet! If we make too much noise, the keepers will come to see what's wrong, and we'll be in trouble. If we want to get free, we have to work together and stay calm."

Eugene shook his head. "This plan won't work. If the keepers come and find us out of our cages, they'll only capture us again, and it will be worse. We should wait until the boat is being unloaded. Then when we get free, we'll be able to escape for good."

Milton swayed from side to side. "That makes sense," he said. "He's right. It would be better to wait."

"Well, I don't want to be in a cage," Lilly said, "but I don't know if I want to be free, either."

The other animals gasped. Eugene stared at her.

"Well, I don't. I never told you about it, Eugene, but for a short while, I lived with a young girl. You remember when she and her parents took me home from the place where we were before? She played with me, took care of me, and gave me food and treats. She was kind, and she let me sleep in a small bed in her room. But then she got sick and went away. Her parents took me back to the store." Lilly looked as if she might cry. "I don't want to be in this cage, but I don't think I want to be 'free' either. I want to be with a little girl again."

"I heard they're sending us to a zoo," said a voice in back, that Bruce thought might have been the snake's.

Another voice said, "I think a zoo is just a bigger cage than this one."

"I don't want to go to a zoo!" several of the animals said at once, and the noise in the room got louder.

Lilly looked at Henry, motioned to him to be calm, and then let out another bark. "Quiet!" she said, and the noise stopped. "I suggest we plan our escape and let these small friends help us get free when the time is right."

"I agree," Bruce said. "Once the boat reaches the dock and your cages are being unloaded, we'll open the doors, and you can go wherever you like."

"I won't come out while those ferrets are loose," said a small voice from the back of the room. They'll eat me!"

"You must all promise to put your instincts aside and concentrate only on helping one another," Bruce said. He pointed to Milton. "This spider would normally eat creatures like me, but we've become friends. You must do the same. You must help one another, or this plan will never work. Can you do this?"

Amid some grumbling, the animals again agreed that they would not eat each other and would help each other as much as possible.

"I guess I should go back in my cage for now," Lilly said, "at least until we reach the island. Can you close the latch again?"

Bruce had no time to respond. They heard heavy footsteps approaching down the hall, and then the door opened with a bang. A large, dirty man, carrying two large sacks that obscured his view of the room, stepped inside. Lilly scooted back into her cage. Bruce scrambled behind Lilly's cage. Milton jumped up next to Henry, who got scared and let out another stink. Bruce hoped Sebastian could get out of the way in time.

"Gah! What is that smell?" the man said, as he dropped the sacks beside the door. "You animals smelled bad before, but that's awful! Good thing we're almost done with this trip. I don't think I could take much more of the smell. They're always at me, saying, 'Go feed the animals, Howard, go clean up the animals, Howard, go feed the animals again, Howard.' This is the last time I have to feed you, and I won't miss you at all. Next stop is the zoo, and the zookeeper can clean up your messes."

The man stopped when he saw Lilly's open cage door. "Now, what have we here? How did your cage get unlocked? That idiot Bill must have left it open. And they say I'm dumb." He shut the door and fastened the latch.

"Ugh! What kind of stuff is that?" Howard said, looking at his hands that had picked up Sebastian's goo. He shook his head, rubbed his hands on his clothing, and set about feeding the animals, mumbling all the time. When he was done, he went out the door, slamming it shut behind him. They heard his footsteps echo down the hallway. When Bruce was sure Howard wasn't coming back again, he climbed up high where the other animals could see him.

"We're figuring out a plan that should work to get you free. We'll tell you what it is soon."

"What do you know about getting us free?" Eugene asked.

"Don't worry," Milton said. "Bruce is a master at finding ways to get his friends out of terrible situations." Milton hopped up and down, getting excited. "If anyone can do it, he can."

Bruce tried to look brave, but he thought that his friends wouldn't be in terrible situations if it weren't for him and his great ideas. He wondered if he really could figure out how to get these animals free before the humans found out what was going on. He hoped he deserved Milton's trust.

Chapter 14

The Taste of Freedom

It was mid-morning the next day when the boat arrived at a new set of docks. Milton ventured outside and reported that there was a hustle and bustle of activity on the part of the men aboard the boat, with many of them moving boxes from the boat to the docks. The animals were excited and restless, wishing the time would come when they would be free of their cages.

There was nothing to do but wait. All the travelers, along with Sebastian, were convinced that the best place they could wait was inside Lilly's cage, so they would be moved to the docks along with her. Bruce and Carly burrowed beneath the straw near the back of her cage. Milton hid in a corner, blending in by means of his natural coloring. Sebastian was sleeping in a different corner, covered by some straw. Bruce thought he would probably sleep through the whole process.

They heard footsteps in the hall.

Several men came into the room and began loading cages onto carts and moving them off the boat. When the men reached the dock, they piled the cages around and on top of one another.

When all the cages had been moved, Carly, Milton, and Bruce crawled onto the dock. Making sure that they stayed out of sight, and hiding when men came by, the three of them unlatched all the cages, one by one. The animals remained inside as they'd agreed, waiting for Lilly to signal the right moment to escape.

Bruce watched until the last of the men had gone back aboard the boat, and then he crawled up Lilly's paw and onto her back behind Carly, who had gripped Lilly's fur in her pincers. Henry flew down and was sandwiched between Carly and Bruce.

When Bruce had a good grip on Lilly's fur, he told Lilly to signal the animals. She let out a loud bark, and the creatures burst from their cages. Bruce watched as all sorts of different animals took off down the dock toward the land. Then suddenly Lilly was also on her way. Bruce was glad he hadn't eaten recently. It was a wild ride!

The men cried out as they saw the animals running down the docks. Some tried to catch the creatures as they sped by, but the animals were too fast. Even the snake moved quickly and was small enough to dart into crevices and around pilings when a human was close to catching him. The parrots took to the sky and began diving at the men who got too close to the animals on the ground.

As they neared the end of the pier, a few men still chased them, but when they reached the road, half of the animals went one way and half the other. The men threw up their hands and turned back toward the boat, shaking their heads.

When the parrots saw the men weren't following any longer, they dipped their wings and flew toward a group of trees in the distance. Lilly's group followed in that direction, and she didn't slow down until she'd also reached the trees. The rest of her group included Eugene, a bobcat, and a young fox. They stayed together in a small circle, panting, trying to slow their breathing, and keeping watch to make sure no one was still following them. It looked as if they were safe for now.

"You can come down now," Lilly said to her passengers.

Henry found his way out of Lilly's fur and flew to a bush, where he sat with a smile on his face.

"Woo-hoo!" Carly said, as she climbed around and hung onto Lilly's side where the ferret could see her. "That was the most fun I've ever had! Can we do it again? Please? Oh, please?"

"Not right now," Lilly said, still trying to catch her breath. "Being cooped up in that cage for so long without exercise has made me flabby. I'm going to have to take a bit of a rest, I think, but maybe we can do it again in a little while."

Carly dropped to the ground and stood looking in admiration at the ferret. Bruce crawled down Lilly's paw.

"That was fun," he agreed, removing his pack and dropping it on the ground. "Scary, but fun. Reminds me of the time we were on Julia's back, remember, Milton?" Bruce looked around for his friend. "Milton?" He didn't see the spider anywhere. "Has anyone seen Milton?"

"Not since we left the cage," Lilly said.

Bruce got a shiver, thinking of Milton alone on the dock. He knew the spider took care of himself quite well, but with so many people milling around and cages being moved, Bruce imagined Milton being taken back aboard the boat and never seeing him again. He felt sick, and his chest ached. How could this have happened? How could he have forgotten his friend?

"I can't leave him there. I have to go back." He looked around at the other animals.

"I'm not going," Eugene said. "I just got away from that cage, and I don't ever want to see it again. Maybe the fox will go."

The fox and the bobcat looked down at their feet. There was a long silence.

Bruce picked up his backpack again and tightened the straps.

"I'll take you," Lilly said. "Climb up. We'll get there faster that way."

Bruce got a lump in his throat. This was so much like the day, long ago, when Meryl had said she would take him to the bat cave. He dipped his head, bowing to the ferret, and began climbing back up her leg. "Thank you," he said. "Both Milton and I can count you as a friend."

"Well, I wouldn't want to be left behind," Lilly said, looking back the way they'd come. "And, yes, I'd like to be your friend." She scowled at Eugene, who looked away.

"I'll come, too," Carly said, starting to climb up Lilly's leg.

"No." Bruce turned to prevent her from climbing further. "You and Henry stay here. You're too young, and I don't want either of you getting caught. Stay here with these friends. They'll protect you." He said the last words as a command, hoping that, in fact, it would be safer for them here.

Carly began to object, but Bruce stood firm. When she realized he wasn't going to change his mind, she backed down and stood watching from the ground.

"I'm ready," Bruce said, getting a good grip. Lilly gave Bruce one quick look and then bounded back down the road to the docks.

She ran like the wind, darting in and out, around and through people's legs, behind packages and crates, under ropes, and over the top of whatever got in her way. She was extremely agile, and it would have been very difficult for any of the men to catch her, even if they'd realized she was there before she was gone.

She reached the boat quickly and stopped behind the empty crates. Her sides heaved in and out as she tried to catch her breath. Bruce looked around but he didn't see Milton anywhere.

"Milton!" he called in a loud whisper. "Milton, are you here?"

No answer.

"Milton!"

Bruce hadn't thought it would be that easy. He crawled up onto the tallest crate and stood on his back legs, straining to see as far as possible. "Milton?"

Suddenly, a dark shape landed next to him. Bruce turned, swiping the air with his claws. He even growled, only to realize it was Milton, who turned a somersault and smiled.

"I knew you'd be back. Thanks for the rescue, both of you. I would have made it down there, you know, but I won't say I mind the assistance, either."

"If you don't stop scaring me like that, I'll leave you behind the next time," Bruce said, hugging his friend. "How did you manage to get left behind?"

"I remembered Sebastian was still asleep in the crate under the straw. I wanted to make sure he didn't end up back on the boat, so I went to wake him, and then you all took off."

Milton led them around the crates to the edge of the dock. Sebastian was there, leaning against a pole. As Milton came closer, Sebastian said, "Ah, the famous circus performer returns! At least, I think you're famous, is that right?"

"Let's get out of here and back to safety," Lilly said. Cocking her head, she smiled at Milton. "Try to stay with us this time, okay?"

"Okay," Milton turned to the snail and bowed. "We have to go back to the circus now, Sebastian. We wish you well and hope we'll see you again the next time the circus comes this way."

Sebastian looked pleased. "Take care, my fine jumping friend. Take care!"

Milton bounded onto Lilly's back, and Bruce climbed up her paw. When both of them were holding tightly, Lilly darted back down the center of the dock and then angled sideways to avoid the obstacles along the way. As she ran, her body rippled up and down, like a small roller coaster on legs. Once he'd gotten used to it, Bruce enjoyed the feeling and the speed. Lilly was very fast.

When she reached the place where they'd stopped before, Lilly let her passengers off and sat down under a tree to catch her breath again. The other animals were still there. Bruce thought they looked ashamed. He was glad.

He glanced around, trying to decide which way to go. He wanted to stay away from people, and he thought it would be best if they could find some other animal to ask about the cooking competition. He had no idea how large the island was, and he didn't want to spend forever searching, if someone could help them find it quickly. On one side of the docks were large buildings and much activity, so he didn't want to go that way. The other side had a road that led past houses and fields and looked much more inviting.

"What do you think?" he said to Milton, gesturing toward the road. "That way look good to you?"

Milton looked in both directions and nodded. "That's the way I'd go. Perhaps we'll run into someone who can give us directions."

"As long as we don't actually run into them," Bruce said with a smile. "Carly, are you ready?"

"I'm tired. I don't have to walk, do I?"

Milton stared at her. Bruce's face took on a serious look. "You're getting pretty big now. You may be the youngest, but you're almost as large as I am. Maybe I should ride on you."

Carly rolled her eyes and made a face. She started practicing stabbing her stinger in the air until she realized that all three traveling companions were staring at her. "You're not serious?"

"No, not now, but if you keep growing, I will be." Bruce took off his backpack and pulled out a leaf. He bit off the stem and held it out for Henry who took it eagerly. "We'll rest here for a while before heading out, okay?"

She nodded. "Yes. I want to know the taste of freedom."

"Okay, then. Let's be off. It is all right if you carry us, isn't it?" Bruce asked.

"Of course. Hang on."

They must have made a strange sight: a caterpillar, a spider, a stink bug, and a scorpion riding on the back of a ferret. A strange sight, indeed.

Chapter 15

The Island

They headed inland and reached the forest by late afternoon. Milton bounced up and down on Lilly's back. "I recognize this area. I'm sure I'm near home now."

Bruce wasn't sure if Milton just wanted this to be the right place or if they really were close to his home. Milton was usually happy and he often had energy he found it hard to contain. He was always bounding ahead, jumping up and down, or swaying from side to side. But this was different. Bruce couldn't be sure what the spider was feeling, but he knew without question that Milton wanted to stop if his family was on the way to the competition.

Bruce thought about how long it would take to do that. The competition would start soon, and he knew it would be easier to get the cookbook if they arrived there ahead of time. That had been his plan, and he wanted to stick to it. If they didn't get there soon, he didn't think they'd be able to pull it off.

"I'm really excited," Milton said. "It will be great for you to meet my family."

Bruce forced a smile. "I hope they like me."

"Of course they'll like you. I can't wait to tell them about our adventures on the last trip and this one so far. If you weren't with me, I know they'd never believe any of it."

"Sometimes I don't believe it myself."

"I know. It seems impossible."

"When I let myself think about what we're doing now, this journey seems impossible, too," Bruce said.

Milton was silent and gazed at Bruce, who was staring off into the distance.

"Then don't think about it. Or think about it this way: if we find my home, great. If we don't, I've had fun being out here with you and Henry and Lilly, and even that little thing," Milton said, pointing to Carly who made a face at him. "I have a family right here, like it or not."

"I like it," Henry said. "I never had a family—well, at least not like you're talking about. My mother laid our eggs and we hatched at the same time, but she wasn't there. I mean, I never really thought about it until now. My brothers and sisters—there were lots of us!—stayed together for a little while. When we were old enough, we flew away and went on our own. I never knew it could be any other way."

"I don't think there's a right or wrong way," Milton said. "And animals are different from insects, I think. I remember watching a bird in one of the trees where I used to hunt. She and her mate made a nest, and after she laid her eggs in it, she sat on those eggs for a long, long time. She didn't even leave to eat, or at least not very often. When the babies were born, they couldn't take care of themselves—not like baby spiders do, or like you, too, I guess. She had to feed them and teach them what to do."

"My mother took care of me like that," Lilly said. She was moving slowly for a change, and her passengers enjoyed the ability to uncurl their legs and just ride without having to hold on so tightly. "I loved it when she would cuddle with my brothers and me. She was warm and soft. But then the woman who cared for us took her away. I still miss her." She yawned. "I'm sorry—I'm not used to being awake so long. I usually sleep a lot during the day and then I'm awake at night. You have a different schedule. I think I'll take a nap for a while, okay?"

Bruce wanted to keep going, but he didn't feel it was right to ask Lilly to continue when she was tired. "Sure," Bruce said. "I'm also kind of tired. Maybe I'll curl up for a little while, too."

They moved under cover of some bushes along the side of the road and settled down for a rest. Bruce knew it would be getting dark soon, so they were probably going to be here for the evening. He saw Milton swaying from side to side, looking off into the distance.

"I'm too excited to sleep right now," he said, when he noticed Bruce looking his way. "I'll take the first watch. Sweet dreams, everyone."

Chapter 16

Searching Again

Henry held very still. Even though this bird was small, it was still much larger than he was, and it had a very long, sharp beak. The bird flew to another tree where it hovered in the air. Henry flew toward Bruce and landed on top of him, jumping up and down on his chest.

"Bruce! Bruce! Wake up!"

"What? What is it?" Bruce said, sitting up and knocking Henry over onto his back. The air already smelled of Henry's stink, and now the little bug let out another. "Aw, Henry—you've haven't done that in a long time! What's the matter?"

"Shh!" Henry whispered, getting back to his feet. "There's a pointy bird in the air by that tree!"

Bruce looked and saw a tiny bird that seemed to be suspended in the air. Its wings beat so fast they were a blur, and they made a loud whirring sound. Suddenly the bird zoomed toward them, flying faster than any bird Bruce had ever seen. As it got closer, he saw that it had a long beak that looked deadly, and he understood why Henry had been afraid.

The bird whizzed by and hovered over a plant that had fuzzy, brown tops. It plucked bits of the fuzz from the plant and held them in its beak. When it flew back the other way, the bird saw Bruce and Henry staring, and it stopped in midair, looking back at them. Bruce backed up, moving Henry behind him. Henry was still pretty stinky, and Bruce couldn't help his face from puckering.

"Ah nah gwah to hur doo," the bird said, with its beak full of fluff. "Ah ee wah wack." It flew to the spot where Bruce had first seen it, and it dropped the fluff into the leaves of a tree. Bruce realized it must be building a nest, and most likely "it" was a "she." The bird flew back and landed on a small branch not far over the travelers' heads.

"I'm sorry for the poor introduction," the bird said, fluttering her wings and tail. "I'm quite busy at the moment, as you can see, but that is no reason to be rude. I didn't mean to scare you, wee one. You can come out. As I said earlier, I'm not going to eat you, and I mean you no harm."

"Pleased to meet you," Bruce said, feeling a little better now, and thinking again about the many different creatures they had met so far.

Henry peeked out from behind Bruce. "Are you really a bird?"

"Yes, I'm a hummingbird. While some hummingbirds eat bugs, this one does not. Filthy habit. All those legs and feelers and wings. I can't imagine stuffing those things into my mouth and trying to swallow them. I'd have to be starving!" She shuddered, fluttering her wings again. "No, I only drink nectar, and I plan to keep it that way." The bird surveyed the rest of travelers who had now awakened and were staring at her. "You're quite the group. I don't recognize you, furry one. What manner of animal are you?"

"I'm a ferret," Lilly said, and she stood on her back legs to show off her fine fur.

"I've heard of ferrets, but you're the first I've ever seen. You're quite beautiful."

Lilly dropped down onto all fours, and Bruce thought she might be blushing, but it was hard to tell under her fur. "Thank you. You're very kind."

"It's been a pleasure talking with you, but I have many things to do and not much time. I'll take my leave, wishing you safe travels and enjoyable days to come."

Bruce suddenly realized that this hummingbird might be a source of information that could help them. "Excuse me—before you go, do you know where the cooking competition is taking place?"

"Oh, yes. In fact, I hope to make my way there tomorrow, if I can finish this nest in time. It's not far from here. If you follow this path, you can't miss it. Continue around the edge of the forest until you come to an old palm tree standing alone. Look beyond it toward the forest, and you will see a building no longer used by humans. That's where the competition is held each year. Are you chefs?"

"No, but we're looking for one who is."

"Well, I wish you the best. I'll be on my way…"

"Please—may I also ask one question?" Milton said, dancing from side to side.

The hummingbird ruffled her wings. "Yes, but please keep it brief. I have many things to do."

"I'm looking for my family. I believe they're on this

island. Have you seen other spiders here who look like I do?"

The hummingbird fluttered her wings. "Well, of course. Many jumping spiders live on the island, and most are not far from here. On your way to the competition, you'll pass a marketplace before you reach the palm tree. Head into the forest behind the marketplace. Someone there should be able to direct you to find your family, as they can't be far."

Milton did a somersault and swayed from side to side, unable to contain his happiness. "Thank you very much! Bruce! We are so close!"

Bruce was happy for Milton, but he was also anxious to get to the competition. He wished they could get the book first and see Milton's family later, but he knew how disappointed his friend would be. Perhaps they could keep the visit very short.

"Well, let's go then," Bruce said, bringing his backpack closer. He pulled a few leaves from a nearby plant, stuffed them into the pack, and then put it on. Yes, he thought, if they had to visit Milton's family first, he was sure he could hurry it up and get on with the search for the cookbook. After all, Milton's family would be there later, but the cookbook might not be.

Chapter 17

Milton's Home

The marketplace was filled with people selling fruits, vegetables, and meats, as well as other items Bruce didn't recognize. People wandered around, picking things up and setting them down. There was more activity here than anywhere Bruce had ever been before.

Milton jumped down and bounded over to one of the crates. "This is where I used to come! It's where I was when I was taken aboard the truck and ended up on the boat!" He was so excited, he made little jumps up and down as he talked. "I know where I am now. I can take you to my home!" He did a double somersault and landed on Lilly's back. "My mother will like you, Lilly. Did I tell you I have lots of brothers and sisters? Mum keeps having babies, and our home is always full of little ones. They're the most fun— always learning and playing."

Despite his desire to keep going, Bruce found himself getting caught up in Milton's enthusiasm, and he knew he would enjoy meeting Milton's family. "Lead the way."

From the marketplace, Milton directed Lilly toward the trees. It was darker here, as the trees cut out some of the light, but it wasn't so dense that they

115

couldn't see. There were bushes Bruce had never seen before, and he wondered if any of them were edible. He wished Angie were there because she would have enjoyed learning about them.

Lilly traveled quickly, but she was wiggling and hopping around a little more than usual. Bruce thought she might be nervous.

"Milton, are there things in this forest that could hurt us?" he asked.

"There are birds, of course, and some cats come this way from the marketplace, but most of them stay there, because there's so much more to eat where the people are. That's one of the reasons I used to go there, too. Then bats come out at night, but we don't have to worry about those right now. A little further on, there's a pond, and we'll have to watch out for the frogs. If we stay on Lilly, there shouldn't be much danger for us, and there aren't any really large creatures in the forest that I know of."

Bruce felt Lilly relax, and he was glad. She'd been very good to them on this trip. Without her help, Bruce knew they would still be making their way back from the docks.

Following Milton's directions, they came to the lake he'd described in a small clearing, with trees around it. The water was a deep blue-black. Bruce saw birds flying over and around the lake, and he was glad for Lilly's presence, since she was large enough to scare the smaller birds away. Large hawks or eagles might find Lilly a tempting morsel, but so far there hadn't been any encounters.

"It's not far now," Milton said. "My home is on the

other side of the lake. You can almost see the tree from here."

Lilly hurried around the lake. Within no time, they reached the area where Milton had pointed.

"Lilly, this is it!" Milton said, and he jumped off and stretched his body. "It might be best if you wait while I go see my Mum and Dad. Once I've explained that I'm in the company of friends, I'll bring you to meet them and the rest of my family."

Bruce remembered the first time his parents met Milton. It had taken them some time to get used to the idea that a caterpillar and a spider could be friends. In this case, it would take a little explaining that Milton's family shouldn't try to eat Bruce, Henry, or Carly, and that Lilly wouldn't be eating them, either.

Milton bounded into the trees and bounced up the trunk of a dark one not far away. He disappeared. Bruce watched the spot where he'd last seen his friend, but Milton didn't come out, so he began talking with Lilly and Carly about the marketplace. Suddenly, out of nowhere, Milton plopped right beside Bruce.

"Aaugh!" Bruce said, leaping away from Milton who had scared him again. Then he made a second huge jump right on top of the spider. Milton was totally unprepared for this, and he fell over, with Bruce on top of him. Bruce stood on top of his friend, holding his legs out to keep Milton pinned. They smelled a familiar odor and knew that Henry had been surprised, too.

"I told you I'd get you for that," Bruce said, grinning, despite the stink that assailed his nostrils and eyes. "You didn't think I could jump like that, huh? Well, I've been practicing. Not like the jumps you make, but fair enough for a caterpillar. Hah!"

"You got me," Milton said with a grin. "That was a good one. Now let me up. This stink is going to kill me!" Milton looked at Henry, who stared at the ground.

Bruce stepped off of Milton's abdomen and looked quite satisfied with himself.

Milton got up and wiped his eyes. "Henry, we have to find a way to stop things from scaring you. But for right now, all of you, come and meet my Mum."

Milton led the way toward the tree, and Lilly followed with Bruce and Carly on her back. Henry flew by himself, trying to keep calm.

When they were almost to the tree, a large brown spider came toward them. "Welcome! Welcome to our home," she said, waving for them to come nearer. As she spoke, Bruce saw hundreds of tiny spiders he hadn't noticed before peeking out from the tree branches and on the ground. They blended so well with their surroundings that he hadn't seen them. He had no idea how many might be out there.

"Are all of these spiders your family?" Bruce asked, wondering how Milton's parents kept track of all of them.

"Yes," Milton said, "although I don't know them yet. They were born while I was gone."

"We can talk about that later," Milton's mother said, still waving toward the tree. "Oh, this is so wonderful! I have a large grasshopper I put away for later and—" She paused. "Ahem. I mean, I can see about finding something special for us to enjoy. Welcome! Welcome all!"

She hopped back onto the tree and pointed with her foreleg, moving several large pieces of loose bark.

"All of the littlest spiders and their father and I make our home here. This is where Milton was born." Her many eyes sparkled. "I'm so happy to see you, my sweet. I never believed you just left home, but I feared the worst, although your father kept saying you'd be back one day. I hate to say he was right, but this time I'm very glad!" Two of her eyes grew moist, and several of the little spiders nestled closer to her. "Most of the older spiders have moved out and live not far from here. Our family is so large now that we have covered most of the local area, and some of your brothers and sisters have moved even further away. I do miss them, but they come back to visit, like you have now, and it's always wonderful to see them. Oh, I wish your father were here! He'll be so happy you're home."

"Where is Dad?" Milton asked.

"He went to the marketplace early this morning. He was looking for larger bugs and planned to bring home a big one, as three of your sisters said they might come by later today." She looked at Bruce and Henry and became flustered again. "But Milton—where are your manners? You haven't introduced your friends."

Milton made the introductions, and each of the friends said "Happy to meet you" or something similar. "I can't introduce all of my sisters and brothers by name, but I can tell you that this is my mum, Fiona. Dad's name is William."

"So tell me about what you've been doing while you were gone," Fiona said. "What kind of mischief have you been into?"

Bruce knew they were in for a long story when Milton began recounting how he had started trying to spin webs in order to catch more prey. Milton's family crept closer and closer while Milton recounted their adventures. Henry and Lilly were also listening, having never heard the entire story before. Even Carly, who normally became bored with everything shortly after it started, was awake and taking in every word.

Bruce's attention wandered, however. He was thinking about the competition and the cookbook, when those around him applauded and cheered. He looked up and smiled at Milton and the others, wondering what they'd been talking about.

"So it was Bruce who got us out of that predicament," Milton said. "He figured out the plan to save us and got the job done. I owe him my life. It's a debt I can't repay, but I'll try."

Bruce became red-faced listening to the praise, especially now, since he knew how little he'd been thinking of his best friend, who was always there by his side and ready to fight for him. He felt terrible.

"What's the matter, Bruce?" Milton's mother asked. "You look like you ate a bug that didn't agree—I mean a bad meal. Are you all right?"

Bruce shook himself and gathered his thoughts around this moment—around his friend's happiness and joyous reunion with his family. "I'm fine. In fact, I'm better than fine. I am the happiest I could possibly be, because my best friend is home with his family, and I'm here with him."

Now Milton was the one to blush. His brothers and sisters poked and jumped on him, and he laughed out loud as he ran around, pretending to try and run away.

Chapter 18

Finding William

Bruce woke with a start, shuddering. In his dream, he'd been lost in a crowd of other insects and animals who were milling around. He couldn't see over them and didn't know where he was going. He tried to move away, but he couldn't get out of the group. When he finally saw an opening, he ran for it, and a large stage came into view. On the stage was a huge praying mantis, and he knew immediately that she was the one they were chasing, the one who had the cookbook. He found himself drawn toward her. He climbed the stairs moved closer. She was bending over a huge pot that hung over a crackling fire. As he came closer, he knew the mantis was going to grab him and plop him in the pot, but he couldn't help himself, and he kept going. When he was close enough, the mantis gestured for him to look into the pot. Knowing it would probably be his last act, Bruce gazed over the rim. There, in the pot, staring at him with huge eyes, was Angie. She reached out, and he started to grab her, when he felt himself rising in the air, the mantis' huge pincers digging into his midsection and back. He watched as Angie got further and further away. He turned and saw the open mouth of the mantis. As she prepared to bite him, he woke up.

121

He had slept in a crevice under the bark of Milton's tree, feeling quite warm and snug until the dream. He couldn't stop shaking now. He climbed down the tree trunk and began walking around, trying to get rid of the horrible feelings. It looked like no one else was awake. He started eating a leaf, thinking if he concentrated on something else like eating, he might feel better. He took a bite and started to chew, but the leaf was the same color as the green mantis in his dream, and he spat it out rather than be sick. He went back to pacing.

When he grew tired, he sat near the base of Milton's tree and looked around. Yesterday had been a very busy day, with the young spiders eager to meet their first caterpillar, stinkbug, scorpion, and ferret. When everyone got to sleep, it was very late, and the moon had been up for quite a while. Now it was still dark, although the sunrise wasn't far off. There was enough light to see shadows and shapes, but not clearly.

The feelings of the dream were beginning to clear when Henry made a loud buzz followed by the usual stink. Bruce thought perhaps he might also have had a bad dream. He didn't have time to think about it, as Henry fell out of the tree and lay on his back on the ground. Squinting, and trying to hold his breath, Bruce helped Henry turn over and get to his feet.

"Are you all right?"

"Yes. I'm sorry," Henry whispered, looking abashed. "I had a bad dream."

"That's okay. I did, too. What was yours about?"

"I dreamed that I was with a lot of other animals and I couldn't make a stink there, but I was scared.

Every time I started to stink, I'd hold it in, but there were so many things that scared me, I puffed up from holding it. I puffed up and up and up until I was huge, and I was almost going to burst, when I woke up."

"You were doing pretty well with your stink for a little while, and then you went back to being scared. What changed?"

The little bug swiveled his feelers and tapped one foot on the ground as he considered his answer. "When it was just you and Milton, I knew you were friends, and I felt safe. I didn't worry much. I knew you liked me, even if I stank. But I don't know Carly or Lilly very well, and now I'm not so comfortable. Carly scares me. I've been holding in the stink sometimes, but I can't always do it. When I get scared enough, it comes out anyway."

"Then we need to find a way to help you feel good again when you start to get scared. We can have you spend some time with Carly, maybe. She's not so scary, really—she just likes to act that way. Hey—I've got an idea. Do you know any jokes or riddles?"

Henry nodded, smiling. "I like silly riddles."

"Okay, then. Here's something to try. The next time you get scared, think about a riddle that you like and say it out loud. Maybe it will take your mind off of whatever was scaring you. Instead, you'll be thinking about us trying to answer the riddle and what the answer is."

Henry thought for a moment. "I'll try it," he said. "Okay, here's one. Why wasn't the mouse a tattletale?"

Bruce couldn't think of a good answer. "I don't know. Why?"

"He didn't want to be a rat," Henry said, grinning.

Bruce groaned. "Oh, no! What have I done? Well, do you feel better?"

Henry marched in place and looked happy. "I do! I hope I know a lot of riddles!"

"Me, too," Bruce said, smiling.

They turned toward a noise coming from the tree above them. It looked as if a spider army was emerging from under the bark of the tree. Spiders were everywhere, greeting each other with "Good morning" or jumping from the tree trunk to the ground and back again. It was chaos, and yet none of them seemed to run into each other. Bruce thought perhaps spiders had an echo sense like bats did.

Milton landed with a plop right between Bruce and Henry. Henry got red in the face and shouted, "What kinds of bugs do firemen dislike?"

Milton stared at Henry. Bruce couldn't come up with an answer. "I don't know."

"Fireflies!" Henry said, and he lifted into the air, flew in little circles around Milton and Bruce, and landed again, twirling in circles on the ground as well. "It worked. It worked!"

"What worked?" Milton said, cocking his head to one side.

"The riddle is like a cure for hiccups, only in this case, it's a cure for the stinks," Bruce said. "I'm glad it's working."

"That makes three of us," Milton said, bouncing up and down.

"Make that four," Carly said, as she crawled out from under a rock.

"Five," added Lilly, who circled around the tree from further in the forest. "That's great, Henry," she said, smiling at the small bug.

"Five what?" Milton's mother asked from the opening under the bark that led to her home.

"Nothing, Mum," Milton said, a smirk on his face.

"Oh, you know I hate it when you do that!" his mother said. "You do it just to irritate me. Well, it's working!" She turned and stalked back under the tree bark.

Milton gave a sheepish grin and bounced up the tree after his mother.

Before Milton could disappear, Bruce hollered, "We should probably think about going to the competition." That reminded him of the gloomy feelings from his dream, but he shook them off. "We'll come back this way after we get the book, okay?"

Milton's smile faded, but he nodded and went inside. Bruce knew Milton wanted to stay longer with his family, but he knew it was also important to get to the competition quickly.

Bruce stuffed the leaf he'd started eating back into his pack.

"Going so soon?" Lilly asked.

"We need to get to the cooking competition and get the owl's cookbook."

"Who's this owl?" Carly asked.

"The owl lives close to my home. His cookbook was stolen, and we need to find it and bring it back. Then he'll help me find my real parents."

Carly looked confused. "Your real parents, huh?

You have other parents who aren't real?"

Bruce shook his head. "No. I have parents, but they didn't make my egg. I'm looking for my egg parents."

"Why? If you have parents where you came from, why . . ."

"Because they only found my egg. I am looking for my real parents—the ones who made my egg."

"But why? If they didn't raise you, it doesn't seem like they wanted you very much."

Carly's words stung as if she'd stabbed him. Bruce scowled. He'd never considered that. He'd thought maybe someone had stolen his egg and left it out in the meadow, or that his egg parents had been forced to leave it there. He never thought that they might not have wanted him.

He thought about Henry and Arlene, his mother and father, and how they had cared for him all these years. His father had told him that his mother had longed for a caterpillar of her own and how happy she was when she found his egg. He said they'd named him Bruce after his great-grandfather, who was loved by everyone.

Bruce was angry and ashamed and hurt. He knew now that he'd been stupid and ungrateful. His "real" parents were the ones he'd left behind. Again.

He thought about this journey and realized he wasn't sure he wanted to keep going. He didn't know if he really wanted to find his egg parents anymore. Maybe it would be better to stay with Milton's family a while longer and then head back home—to his "real" home.

He started to climb the tree and tell Milton what he was thinking when the spider appeared, a worried look on his face.

"Mum's upset. You know, Dad didn't come back last night, and he was supposed to be here yesterday afternoon. He's never been late like this before, and she's worried that something's happened. She asked if we'd go look for him."

"Sure," Bruce said, still scowling, thinking this settled it. They would go find Milton's father and then come back here. Later, when the time was right, Bruce would leave and go back home. "You said he went to the marketplace?"

"Yes. That has me worried, too. That's where I was when I ended up on the boat."

"Let's hope that didn't happen. Don't worry—I'm sure he's fine, and we'll find him coming home while we're on our way there."

"Hope so," Milton said, but he still looked worried.

"I'm ready," Lilly said, yawning, and she stretched out her paw for Bruce. He put on his pack, climbed up, and held onto the fur behind her head. Henry flew and landed in front of him, digging down into her fur to keep out of the wind. Carly walked up Lilly's leg and positioned herself behind Bruce, grasping Lilly's fur in her pincers and lying as low as possible. Milton jumped up on top of Lilly's head where he could guide her on the right path.

Milton's mother came out to see them off. She rubbed her front feet together and kept looking off into the distance. Bruce looked, too, but there was no sign of Milton's father anywhere.

"Don't worry, Mum. We'll find him, and we'll be back soon." His mother didn't say anything, but she waved one leg, and Milton asked Lilly to go. She started slowly and then gained speed, until she was running down the path to the marketplace.

It took very little time to get back there, even with all of them calling out when they saw a spider who might be Milton's father.

When they reached the stalls at the marketplace, they were careful to stay away from the people. They called for William as they went through the market, but he didn't answer. They made the circuit for the second time.

"Dad! Are you here?"

A small voice said, "Are you looking for a spider?"

"Yes! Who are you? Have you seen him?"

"Agatha took him." A tiny vole peeked out of a crevice at the back of one of the stalls. "She took him to the competition."

"Who is Agatha? Why would she take my Dad to the competition?"

The vole just looked at Milton. "He's your Dad? I'm sorry."

Milton jumped down and landed in front of the vole, who scooted back into the crevice. "Why? Why are you sorry?" Milton shouted.

The vole didn't come out but spoke very quickly. "I'm s-sorry because, at the competition this year, the specialty is spiders."

Milton swayed from side to side. "What do you mean, 'the specialty is spiders'?"

"If you'll back up and promise not to hurt me, I'll explain," the vole said.

Bruce had climbed down to be near his friend, and

he touched Milton's leg, motioning for him to back up a little. Milton stepped backward and waited, swaying from side to side, until the vole poked his head out.

"Every year, the judges choose a specialty for the cooking competition. This year it's spiders. Even though the animals and insects who attend are sometimes chosen as the main dish, that's the way it is in the world, you know? Fish eat flies and birds eat fish; caterpillars eat leaves and are eaten by birds who are eaten by cats. It's not good or bad—it's just the way things are. Anyway, this year, Agatha wanted to find a nice, big spider for her main dish. She had us looking for three days. I found him yesterday morning and sent word. She came down, caught the spider, and left for the competition right after that."

Milton looked like he was going to be sick.

"But you didn't answer the other question," Bruce said. "Who is Agatha?"

The vole drew back a little. "Agatha is the chef who usually wins the competition. Agatha is a praying mantis."

Chapter 19

The Competition

The friends didn't waste any time before heading to the competition. Lilly was running at top speed, and the travelers gripped tightly to make sure they didn't slip off.

Milton stayed up near her head, keeping a lookout with his many eyes. Bruce could tell he was still upset by the way he held himself stiffly, and he wished there was something he could do to help. They were doing all they could.

They rounded a bend on the road and saw the huge palm tree. This had to be the place to turn. Lilly stopped near it, panting. The travelers got down to give her a chance to rest for a short while. Bruce looked toward the trees and thought he saw the shape of a building when a centipede appeared, carrying a large parcel on his back. Spotting Lilly, he shied away, lay on his side, and curled into a circle.

"We won't hurt you, centipede," Bruce said. "We're busy with other things."

The centipede uncurled a little and raised his head. "Never can be too careful," he said, uncurling a bit more. When he'd straightened out, he stood and started walking away from them toward the building.

"G'day to you, then," he said over his shoulder.

"Nice day for it, don't you think?"

"For what?" Bruce asked, following slightly behind and trying to catch up. He wasn't feeling like it was a very nice day at all. That feeling didn't change when Henry landed on his head.

"For the competition, of course," the centipede said. "The biggest event of the year. Everyone either wants to win or has someone they hope will win. But I need to get there quickly. I was supposed to be there early this morning. I'm delivering the megaphone for the announcer. Who's your pick for this year's winner?"

Bruce suddenly thought this centipede might be able to help them get into the competition. He motioned for the others to follow and then he sped up until he was side by side with the centipede.

"We hope it will be Agatha, of course. In fact, we're going there to meet her. She asked us to bring some ingredients for her main dish. We must hurry, too."

"Bruce, that's not tr—" Henry began, but Bruce reached up and poked him.

"Would you like to join us? You'd get there more quickly," Bruce said, turning to look at Lilly. He thought she might have looked unhappy at having yet another passenger, but she said nothing.

"Hmm. I'd say you have a rather full group now. Do you think there's room for one more?"

"Oh, we can make room for you. I'd hate to have you have to walk, when we can carry you there more quickly. You don't want to be late with the megaphone, right?"

"Well, if you think I'll fit," the centipede said, and he moved closer as Lilly hesitantly extended her paw.

131

He climbed up and found a spot on her back behind the others. Lilly shivered just a little.

"This will be interesting," he said. "I've never ridden on a—just what are you?"

"A ferret," Lilly said. "Are you ready or will we be waiting for anyone else?"

Bruce was sorry he'd invited the centipede without asking her, but he thought it was necessary. "We're ready, Lilly."

Everyone held tightly to her fur and she bounded off toward the forest along the path.

"So," Bruce said, "you are one of the officials at this competition?"

"Not an official, but one who likes to be of help. I run errands for the contestants and for those in charge. They let me in free, and I enjoy meeting the chefs."

"You must know Agatha, then?"

"I've seen her once or twice, but never up close. She usually has her own insects helping her. Like you."

"Of course," Bruce said. "But this is our first time at the competition. She hired us to replace some beetles who couldn't be here this year."

"Well, I'm surprised at her hiring the spider, given that they're this year's specialty."

Bruce thought quickly. "It was a last-minute decision when the beetles got sick. We were the only ones available."

"You're the lucky ones, then! Look—that's the building. If you go around to the side where the large bushes are, you'll see an entrance for the competitors and the crew. That's where you go in. Give the guard the password and he'll let you pass."

This was exactly what Bruce had hoped for. "Yes, well, that's our problem. When we were getting ready to leave, Agatha told us she needed to give us information about how to get in, but in the hurry of the last-minute preparations, she forgot. I don't think she remembered this was our first time here."

Lilly stopped running and walked at a regular pace toward the bushes the centipede had indicated.

"That's easy, then," the centipede said. "Just say 'dumpling' and he'll let you in."

Bruce beamed. Lilly stopped and extended her paw. The centipede was the first to crawl to the ground. When Carly started after him, Bruce held her back.

Seeing that the others didn't follow, the centipede turned and asked, "Aren't you coming?"

"We will, but we need to gather some things first and make sure we have everything we need before going in," Bruce said. "We'll see you there soon."

"All right," the centipede said. "Thanks for the ride."

The centipede walked toward the entrance and was met by a large rat who stood in the way. The rat said something, the centipede replied, pointed to the parcel on his back, and the rat let him pass.

Bruce looked at the building. It was in sad shape. The plaster on the outside was crumbling. The roof had fallen in a few places, and there were pieces of rubble around the outside. He wondered what had happened to cause the men to abandon this building.

"What are we waiting for?" Milton asked. "What are these things we need to gather?"

"We're not gathering anything," Bruce said. "I said

that so he would go in first, and we could follow alone." Bruce started climbing down and the others followed. "Once we're inside, we'll try to find Agatha. Henry and Carly—I want you to stay out of sight until I know it's safe for you to be with us. Once I know what we're up against, I can make a plan. Lilly—will you wait outside for us? Be ready to go, though, as we may need to get away quickly. Okay?"

Lilly, who was licking her fur to clean it, nodded.

"I want to come with you to look for Agatha," Henry said.

"Me, too," Carly said, waving her tail.

"It would be better if you wait," Bruce said, and Milton nodded. "Henry, you've been good about not stinking, but on this trip, it's important that we're not seen—or smelled—unless we want to be. And Carly—you're getting bigger, but I want you to wait with Henry."

Henry pouted a little, but he didn't ask again. Carly pouted a lot.

"You two will come with us until I find a safe place for you to hide. Milton, let me do the talking when we get there." They began walking toward the building.

When they reached the doorway, the rat looked them over and sniffed the air, wrinkling his nose. "You can't come in here. Go around to the front of the building." He stood on his hind legs and folded his arms. Bruce knew he did this to make himself look larger and more powerful. It was working.

Bruce didn't think asking nicely would get them in the door. He scowled and spoke in a gruff voice.

"We're here to deliver some stuff to Agatha."

"To Agatha? No. I know Agatha's hired help, and

you're not it. Get outta here before I kick you out."

"She's not gonna like it when she finds out her cooking was ruined because of some rat who wouldn't let us in. But, if you insist." Bruce shrugged his shoulders and turned around. "Come on, everyone. We get a day off instead of having to work."

The rat's eyes darted around and he frowned. He looked into the doorway and then back to the travelers who were gathered near Lilly's paw.

"Wait." The rat's face took on a superior appearance and he smiled, although it looked more like a sneer. "I'll let you in if you know the password, but I don't think you do."

Bruce turned and walked back to the rat. He stood as tall as he could. "Of course I know the password. It's 'dumpling.'"

The rat's eyes opened wide and then he scowled again. "Go in, then," the rat said, gesturing to the door. "Turn left and head down the hall. Go on, and make it snappy! You're holding up the line."

Bruce saw several other insects and animals behind them who were fidgeting in line.

"On our way," Bruce said. He waited for the others to catch up and then scurried through the entrance into the corridor on the other side.

The hallway was quite wide, and he saw a door at the end. He turned to make sure everyone had come in with him. His mind suddenly recalled moments in the cave on their last adventure, moments when he had been afraid, and he started feeling that way now. He hadn't let himself think too much about what they were going to do before this—he knew that if he thought about it too much, he might not go through with it. That wasn't an option now. They weren't looking for the cookbook. They were here to find Milton's father.

They reached the door which had been propped open with a rock. Bruce put his head through and looked around. He didn't see anyone, so he signaled the others to follow. They came into a large room that contained some old pieces of wood and other items Bruce didn't recognize. Mostly it was full of dust and dirt. They continued straight ahead toward some doors at the end of the room. As they moved forward, Bruce heard noises—animals chattering and insects buzzing—through another set of doors to their right. These doors were also propped open, and the sounds grew louder as they got closer. Bruce was turning to look through the doors, when a group of stinkbugs came running through and smacked right into him. He fell over sideways, and they plopped in all directions. Of course, one or two of them let out a stink.

"What kind of tree has the best bark?" Henry blurted out.

"Not now, Henry!" Bruce sputtered, trying to clear away the acrid odor as he disentangled his legs from those of the stinkbugs and stood up again.

"A dogwood," Henry whispered, more to himself than anyone else. Bruce scowled at him.

"I'm sorry," one of the other stinkbugs said. She was smaller than Henry, but had a coloring similar to his. Some of the others were shades of brown or red or had stripes. "We shouldn't have been running. I hope you're all right."

"I'm fine. Just shook me up a little. Where are you headed so fast?" Bruce asked.

"We need to fly back to the marketplace to get something," the bug said. "It's a long way, and I don't know if we'll make it in time." She turned and the others followed her, walking as quickly as they could toward the doorway. "I'm sorry, but we have to go."

"Wait! Before you go, perhaps you could make it up to me by telling me where Agatha is and where she's keeping her meal preparations?"

"Agatha and all the contestants are on the stage, setting up their cooking areas. Their meal preparations are stored in rooms on the other side of the building. I don't know which room is hers. Some of them share a space, although I think Agatha has her own room since she's won so many competitions."

"Zoe, we have to go!" said one of the other stinkbugs. Zoe turned, and the bugs began dashing away again. Henry watched them with a wistful look.

Bruce looked for a place where Carly and Henry could wait, but after seeing the area, he thought it might be best if they stayed in one group.

"Okay," he said, standing tall and trying to seem brave. "Act like you know what you're doing, like you belong here. Let me do the talking. Don't look around too much. Pretend that you are supposed to be here and look busy. Oh—and stay together. I don't want to lose any of you."

Carly looked smug and flicked her tail this way and that as she walked behind Bruce.

Chapter 20

The Mud Ball

hey marched through the door, looking as official as possible. They couldn't help glancing around a little, although they tried to make it seem inconspicuous. Bruce counted nine cooking stations, set up in three rows of three stations, each with a different animal or insect tending to preparations. At the back, closest to where they came in, were the largest animals: a rat, a lizard, and a gerbil. In front of them were a mouse, a frog, and a finch. In the front row, nearest the audience, were a wasp on one side, a spider on the other, and directly in the center was Agatha, the mantis. Bruce guessed that she had the place of honor front and center, despite her large size, because she was last year's competition winner. He didn't see William anywhere. He thought, if Agatha stayed on the stage, he could get to her storeroom, wherever it was, and find William without her even knowing.

"Arthur—I asked you to bring me dandelions." Agatha was placing white flower petals into the outstretched forelegs of a small, red-faced grasshopper. "These are daisies. Dandelions are the yellow flowers. Now go out and bring me some dandelions."

She patted Arthur on the head and turned away

138

from the little bug, who scurried away and ran past Bruce, dropping white petals as he hurried by.

"Best not to let them get away with those kinds of mistakes," Agatha continued, smiling at the small audience that had assembled in front of her. "Arthur's parents sent him to me for an education, and an education he will get."

Bruce headed toward the other side of the stage and the door he could see there. He noticed that the roof was gone over this part of the auditorium, letting in light, and he wondered what the contestants would do if the weather turned bad. He chided himself for the stray thoughts that kept coming into his head, telling himself to concentrate on finding William.

When he reached the door, Bruce checked that everyone was still with him. Henry was riding on Milton who brought up the rear, right behind Carly. Bruce had never seen Milton so quiet. He didn't seem sad or upset. It was like an emptiness had settled in him. Truly, all of them seemed very quiet, and not only because they wanted to get safely across the stage without making noise. It was something deeper. Bruce fought to keep his thoughts focused.

They reached the doors at the far end of the stage, and Bruce looked through the opening. To the right was a corridor with doors leading off on both sides. He motioned for the others to follow and headed down the hall. The first door was open and he peeked in. Two mice were inside. He thought they might be with the other mouse who was cooking on stage.

"Excuse me," Bruce said. "Can you tell me which room belongs to Agatha?"

"End of the hall," the mice chirped together.

Bruce thanked them and headed down the hall. A few of the other doors on the way were open, and Bruce glanced inside, not seeing anything of interest.

They found the door to the last room partially open like the others. Bruce peeked inside. A salamander with her back to them was digging through a box and talking to herself. Bruce was reminded of the first time he saw Angie mumbling about seeds behind the tree. He didn't see Milton's father.

Bruce backed out of the doorway. "Wait out here, all of you, while I talk with this salamander." Bruce was surprised when they did as he asked without complaint. He put his head back in the doorway to Agatha's room.

"Ahem."

"Can I help you?"

"Agatha sent me to bring the spider, but I don't see him here."

"Who are you?" The salamander squinted at Bruce and cocked her head to one side. He knew she didn't believe him. He'd have to act tough again.

"Doesn't matter who I am. What matters is that I get that spider to her now, and that you don't make me late. Where is he?"

The salamander looked unsure and started to move past Bruce.

"Fine. Take time to check it out. I can't wait until Agatha sees you coming and the spider isn't there."

She stared at Bruce. Narrowing her eyes, she said, "He's in the next room. Now let me get back to what I was doing."

Bruce decided it wouldn't hurt to ask about the cookbook, since she was giving him information. "Oh, Agatha also needs her cookbook. One of the other contestants made a bet with her about something, and she says the proof is in the book."

"If she didn't tell you where it is, I can't help you. When you bring the spider, ask her where she put the book." The salamander turned her back on Bruce and started poking through the box again.

Bruce backed out the door. His heart was beating fast and hard. He nearly bumped into Carly who was right behind him.

"I didn't know you could lie like that," she whispered. "You're very good at it."

Bruce scowled but said nothing. He looked around, but Henry was nowhere to be seen. The door to the next room was closed, but there was a space beneath it, and Milton was crawling under it. At that moment, Henry flew toward them from across the hall, shaking his head. "No William there." From behind the door, he heard Milton groan.

"Henry, come with me. Carly, stay here and keep a lookout. If you see or hear anyone coming, make a noise we'll hear, and then crawl under the door. Okay?"

"Sure."

Bruce scurried under the door, and Henry was not far behind. Milton stood on his back legs in the center of the room. His front feet rested on a huge ball of dried mud. There was a small hole near the top of the ball, but otherwise it was completely round.

"I'm in here!" said a voice from within the ball.

"Get me out! The mantis said she planned to roast me in this thing—that it would keep me juicy. That's her secret for winning the cooking contest year after year!"

"We'll get you out, Dad!"

Bruce couldn't believe Milton's father was in the mud ball. He tapped on the outside of it. The mud was very hard. He looked around the room for something that might break through it, but he didn't see anything. Then he had a thought. He went to the door and called underneath.

"Carly? Come here."

She scooted under the door. "What's that?" she said, looking at the mud ball. She moved toward it and banged on it with her claw.

"Don't do that!" William said from within the ball.

"Whoa. Who's in there?"

"My dad is in there!"

"Carly, do you think you can chip him out of there?" Bruce asked. "Could you use your stinger to pierce a hole in the mud and break it up?"

"Might work. I'll try." She moved close to the ball, brought her tail up over her back, and stabbed the ball with her stinger.

Carly had grown quite a bit, and the point made a dent in the clay, but it wasn't strong enough to do more than that. She tried a few more times, but it didn't work.

"Sorry," she said, backing up and crawling under the door.

Bruce looked disappointed, and he began pacing back and forth. "We need to find something stronger to break the ball. Did any of you see something that might work? There has to be..." Bruce continued pacing until he got an idea. "I know! Remember the stream we passed on the way here? If we can get the ball into the shallows of that stream, the water would dissolve the mud. It might take a little while, but we could probably help it along by digging into it after it starts to soften."

Carly scooted under the door into the room again. "Someone's coming!"

The room became hushed. They heard a scuttling in the hall outside. The sound continued past the door. Then they heard Agatha's voice coming from her room at the end of the hall.

"Did you find the herbs?"

"Not yet. We may need to gather more."

"They're here. Keep looking."

"I am."

"Here, I'll help. Have you been through this box?"

Bruce knew they didn't have much time before Agatha would come to get William. "Can we roll this ball?"

Milton pushed, and it rolled, although they saw a flat spot where the ball had rested on the floor.

"What are you doing?" William said.

"Dad, be quiet! Were getting you out of here." Milton continued rolling the ball toward the door.

Bruce poked his head beneath the door. He didn't see anyone, so he motioned for the others to go through. Carly scurried out, followed by Henry. Bruce helped Milton roll the ball, trying to push it through the space under the door. The opening wasn't large enough.

"Milton—turn the ball so it's back on the flat spot. It won't be as tall that way, and maybe we can push it under the door."

Milton rolled the ball around until it sat on the flat spot in front of the door. Bruce wasn't tall enough to see the top of the ball, but he thought it might fit.

They pushed and pushed, but the ball wouldn't slide. Milton frowned, swaying from side to side. Bruce tried to think of some way to make the floor slippery. He remembered he had some shiny leaves in his pack. He thought if they put the ball on top of those leaves, it might slide more easily.

He explained his idea, and Milton rolled the ball off the flat spot. Bruce pulled the leaves out of his pack and put them where the ball had rested before. Milton rolled the ball back until it sat on top of the leaves.

"One more time," Bruce said, and he began to push. Milton joined in, and the ball moved forward slightly. They pushed harder, and the ball continued moving, slowly. When it was a little more than halfway under the door, the pushing got easier, and Bruce saw that the flooring outside the room was different and shinier. The ball slid easily the rest of the way. Bruce smiled at Milton, but he still looked worried.

Bruce's happiness vanished when he heard Agatha's voice again at the end of the hall. He looked that way and could see her tail moving through the open door.

"I didn't ask anyone to bring the spider. I'm not ready for him yet."

"You didn't send a caterpillar here earlier?"

"Caterpillar? No. Why?"

144

"Hurry!" Bruce whispered loudly. "Go! Roll the ball down the hall and out the door!"

Milton pushed the mud ball, trying to avoid the flat spot that made a thunk every time it hit the floor. Bruce wanted to tell him to go faster, but he knew that his friend was doing the best he could. Henry flew above Carly, who followed Milton down the hall.

Bruce turned again and saw Agatha moving backward into the hall. His heart sank, and he began running to catch up with the others. Milton had the mud ball rolling quite fast now. Bruce ran even faster and managed to catch up to Milton, who was struggling to keep the mud ball rolling the way he wanted it to go. Bruce moved ahead to the corner and looked around. A group of mice, carrying baskets, were chattering to one another and not paying attention. Bruce yelled, telling them to move out of the way, but they just stood and looked.

The mud ball came rolling toward the corner. Milton had pushed it so fast that he couldn't make the turn. The ball bounced off the wall, but Milton was able to push it through the opening to the stage and toward the mice standing there. They stood, staring wide-eyed, as the ball careened toward them.

Bruce leaped in front of the ball and pushed the mouse closest to him away from it and toward the others, knocking them out of the way. Milton got the ball back under control and continued rolling it along the back of the stage toward the hall where they'd come in.

"I'm sorry," Bruce yelled to the mice, as they tried to get up from the pile. They seemed to be okay, if a little shaken up. But as he looked back toward them, he saw Agatha stalk around the corner.

"Stop! You'll never get away!" she cried, racing toward them through the opening. "Thieves! They've stolen my spider! Stop them!"

Bruce knew she would catch them before they could reach the hallway. He looked around and saw a curtain at the back of the stage.

"Milton, push the ball under the curtain!"

He didn't know what was back there, but he thought it might give them time to figure out what to do. He hoped it would be dark, and perhaps mantises couldn't see well in the dark.

Milton gave the ball a push toward the curtain. It slid underneath, and he disappeared after it.

"Henry, Carly, follow Milton!" Bruce stood by the curtain, waiting for them to go through.

Instead, Henry lifted off of Carly's back and flew overhead, keeping an eye on Agatha. Carly simply stopped. When Agatha approached the curtain, Carly moved toward the mantis, raising her tail over her head in a threatening gesture.

"No, Carly! You're too little. She'll eat you!" Bruce cried, willing her to come back to the curtain.

"Go on," Carly said, her voice calm and hard. "Get everyone to safety." She never took her eyes away from Agatha. "Listen, mantis—don't come any closer, or I'll sting you with my poison. It's not a pleasant way to die."

A movement above caught Bruce's eye. Henry was flying toward the mantis from behind. When he passed her face, he let go of an enormous stink. Acrid droplets flew into Agatha's face. She shrieked and rubbed her forelegs over her eyes.

"Come on!" Bruce said, holding the curtain up. Henry landed on Carly's back again, and she slid beneath it. Bruce slipped through, hoping no one would chase them now. He couldn't believe the two of them had stood up to the mantis, who was so much larger than they were.

It was darker behind the curtain, but some light came through a door that was partially open at the back. Milton had pushed William's mud ball nearly to that door. Carly hurried to catch up to him, and Bruce followed. Nearing the door, he saw a satchel on the floor behind a small pile of boxes. Sticking out of the satchel was a large book. His heart quickened. He stopped and pulled the book from the satchel, revealing the cover. "My Winning Recipes." Bruce couldn't believe it. This had to be the cookbook he'd been searching for. The book was large, though, and he knew he'd have trouble carrying it alone. He called Carly back. She had grown so much that he thought she might be able to hold it in her claws. She picked up the book and scooted out the door. Bruce scrambled after her and then chased after Milton, who had rolled the mud ball into an open field.

Chapter 21

The Chase

ilton guided the mud ball onto a small path that ran behind the theater. Rocks and sticks sometimes made the ball stop, and he would have to push it sideways and start it rolling again. Bruce realized Milton couldn't see over the top of the ball, so he couldn't avoid things in his path. Bruce asked Henry to fly above and call out directions.

"Toward me," Henry said, and Milton pushed the ball to the left. "Not that far," Henry said, as the mud ball hit a rock and stopped.

Milton looked exasperated and wiped a foreleg across his eyes. "Henry, give me more information, so I don't keep hitting things, okay?"

"I'm doing the best I can," Henry said, looking hurt.

Milton sighed, as Henry landed on top of the mud ball.

"I know you are, but—"

"Shh!" Henry whispered.

"I'm only trying to—"

"No, really! Shh!"

Everyone was quiet. Bruce heard a faint sound, like someone calling for help. He moved closer and realized it was coming from the mud ball.

"It's your father!" Bruce said. Looking at the mud ball, he realized the flat spot was near the top, and the small hole that allowed William to breathe wasn't visible. "Turn the ball over! Find the breathing hole!"

Milton pushed the ball sideways, away from the rock, and then onto the flat spot. A large gasp sounded from the hole, followed by another. Then a very quiet, "Thank you."

"I'm so sorry, Dad!" Milton said, rocking from side to side and rubbing his forelegs together. "I'll be more careful from now on. Are you okay?"

"I'm dizzy from the rolling and bumping, and perhaps from the lack of air, but that's better now, thanks. Are we near the stream?"

"Almost," Milton said, although they still had quite a way to go. "Ready to go again?"

"There they are!" shrieked Agatha from behind them.

Bruce turned and saw the mantis pointing at them. His spirits sank, as he realized Agatha was still chasing them. He'd hoped she might decide that finding a new spider for her main course would be easier than chasing William, but he'd been wrong.

"And they have my cookbook, too! Get them!" Agatha shouted. She was surrounded by several large rats who ran as a pack, charging toward Bruce and his friends, and Agatha wasn't far behind.

"Run! Fly!" Bruce turned from his pursuers and began climbing the nearest tree. He didn't know if rats could climb, but he hoped not. Carly clambered up the tree behind him, still holding the cookbook.

Bruce was about halfway up, when he looked back

and saw the rats were nearly upon them. He spotted Milton, who had climbed a different tree. He didn't see Henry, but he assumed the little bug was flying and would be safe.

The rats reached the base of Bruce's tree and started climbing, when a brown, furry shape knocked the rats over with a growl. There was a tangle of rats and the brown animal, a fighting mass of teeth and claws and flying fur. It was Lilly!

The growling and hissing stopped, and the tangle drew apart. The rats, some of them bloody, backed away from Lilly, who stood guarding the base of the tree. Agatha moved closer and stood next to William's mud ball.

"Give me the cookbook, I'll take back this spider, and you can go your way. Keep up this nonsense, and I will send others who are larger and more powerful to hunt you down and take back what is rightfully mine."

"My father is in that mud ball. I will not let you take him back." Milton's tone was stronger and more determined than Bruce had ever heard before.

"And I will not give you the cookbook, because you stole it from someone else, and I'm taking it back to its rightful owner," Bruce said.

"That is a lie!" Agatha said, pointing at Bruce, and flaring her wings. She was terrifying. "The cookbook is mine. Open the cover and read what it says. 'My Winning Recipes by Agatha Moss.' I am Agatha Moss!"

Bruce didn't believe it. He motioned for Carly to open the book so he could see inside. Agatha was telling the truth. Her name was there on the first page.

How could the book belong to Agatha when Conrad told him she stole it from the owl? If the book was Agatha's, then Conrad lied, and if he lied, then Bruce had stolen the book from Agatha. He squirmed. He knew he had to give the book back to Agatha, but if he didn't bring it to the owl, how would he learn anything about his egg parents?

Bruce looked at Milton who was moving from side to side. He shook his head. He was being selfish again. The book didn't matter. The only thing that mattered was Milton's father in the mud ball.

"We didn't know the book was yours, and I'm sorry about taking it," Bruce said. "Someone asked us to fetch it. He told us it belonged to him, and that you had stolen it. We'll give you the cookbook, but we won't leave without the spider. You'll have to find a different main dish."

Agatha looked angry and rocked her head from side to side. "I don't approve of your methods, but I'll agree, since I must have my cookbook, and I don't have time to argue. The competition begins soon. Now I suppose I must catch and prepare a new spider. You've caused me a great deal of upset. Drop the book, and I will leave this spider to you." She backed away from the mud ball, staring at Carly and Bruce.

Bruce had the beginning of an idea. "Agatha, we never intended you harm. We thought we were doing something right, and it turned out to be wrong." He paused, trying to collect his thoughts. "But if I don't bring your book to the owl who sent us here, I cannot fulfill my part of a bargain that would help me learn something I need to know. Would you be willing to help me get that information?"

"Why would I help you? You have made my life very difficult. I have no time for this. Give me my book and go away."

"But we can help each other. If I help you now, will you help me after the competition?"

"I don't need your help. What could you do for me?"

"I can help you . . ." But Bruce realized he didn't have any idea what he could do for Agatha. He had nothing she needed. He looked down and said, "There must be something I can do."

"Would you like to be my new main dish?" Agatha said, looking straight at Bruce. When he didn't reply, she continued, "Never mind. I don't have a good recipe for caterpillar, anyway." Agatha jerked her forefoot and pointed to the ground. "Drop the book!"

Bruce had a flash of inspiration. "Listen! I do have something to offer you. Something that will be of great help to you."

"I don't have time for this! Spit it out. I'm late as it is."

"You don't have a main ingredient for your recipe, right? What if I share with you a recipe that requires no animal or insect of any kind, and yet is one of the tastiest meals I've ever eaten? I believe you would already have most of the ingredients you'd need to make it. I know the recipe by heart, because I used to help my mother prepare it every time we had a special occasion. It's her family secret, but I'm sure that she wouldn't mind if I share it with you now. Here's my bargain: If you like my recipe, then you'll help me after the competition. If you don't, you'll have your book back, and we'll leave."

Agatha tapped the tips of her front feet together. She looked at the mud ball, then at Lilly, and said, "All right. I doubt your recipe will be of use, and I've never cooked without some sort of meat or insect in my main dishes, but I'll listen. Make it snappy!"

Bruce began listing the ingredients that were needed for his mother's mushroom and barley stew, and he explained the directions needed to put the dish together.

Agatha tipped her head first to one side and then the other, and she rubbed her forefeet together. "Interesting. Sounds delicious. No meat or insect needed. Well, that certainly would save time, but I don't have any of the mushrooms you mentioned, and I don't know where to find any in such a short time."

"We can help with that," Bruce said. "I spotted some as we were heading this way. It shouldn't take us long to gather them and bring them to you."

Agatha rubbed her forefeet together, pondering the idea. "We have a deal," she said, and then she raised her front legs in the air. "I probably should have asked what kind of help you need from me before agreeing so quickly."

"Nothing too much," Bruce replied, hoping that was true. "But come on—let's get those mushrooms!" He nodded to Carly to drop the book. It fell next to Lilly, who backed away. Agatha strode forward, picked up the book, and headed back up the path to the theater. The rats turned to follow, but not without giving dirty looks to the travelers before following her.

Bruce hadn't realized how scared he'd been facing the mantis and the rats. Any one of them would have made a meal of all of them without even blinking. If it hadn't been for Lilly, they all—well, all except perhaps Henry—would be dead for sure.

Bruce climbed down from the tree and discovered his legs were shaky. "Lilly, I don't know what to say except thank you. If you hadn't come when you did, we'd be—"

"You're welcome," Lilly said, "but there's no need for thanks. You'd have done it for me."

"You're not hurt, are you?"

Lilly shook her head.

"Good." Bruce thought for a moment. "How did you know we were here and needed help?"

"I heard some loud, strange voices on the other side of the building, and I decided to see what was going on. I saw Milton rolling this ball and all of you running after. Then I saw the praying mantis and the rats, and I realized you were in trouble. I ran around through the trees, staying out of sight, until you all began climbing. I circled around behind you and figured I'd come out when the time was right."

"I'm glad you did," Bruce said. "Of course, now I need to ask if you'd take us to find those mushrooms again—the ones we saw when we headed this way."

"Sure will." She cocked her head toward the mud ball and said, "What is that?" as she extended her front leg for Bruce and Carly to climb up.

Bruce explained about finding Milton's father and getting him out of the theater, as well as finding the book.

"How are you going to get William out of the mud ball?" Lilly asked.

"We plan to dunk him in the stream until the mud softens."

"Then let me carry the ball to the stream, drop it off there, and continue with you to get the mushrooms. Milton can stay and help his father get free, while you and Carly help gather mushrooms with me."

"Wonderful!" Bruce said, as he and Carly climbed up her paw and settled themselves on her back. Milton jumped up, as Lilly picked up the mud ball in her mouth, and Henry settled on Carly's back.

"Ib ebryboby rebby?" Lilly said.

"Yes! I'm ready!" came a small voice from inside the mud ball.

The travelers laughed, and Lilly started on her way.

Chapter 22

Cooking

It didn't take long to find the spot where the mushrooms grew on the side of the path. They were plentiful, growing in the shade of two large almond trees amid grass and mosses not far from the stream. Lilly had dropped William's mud ball at the edge of the water, and Milton rolled the ball this way and that, trying to soften the mud enough for his father to get free.

As they gathered mushrooms, Bruce said, "Carly, what were you thinking back there in the building when Agatha came out? Threatening to sting her. You could have been killed! We haven't brought you all this way to see you eaten."

Carly stopped gathering and looked at Bruce. "I never intended to stick around long enough to actually poke her. Besides, I don't think I could have found the right spot between those hard things on her body. I was bluffing. I thought it would give you some time to get Milton's father away." She started picking mushrooms again. "You know, I learned it from you."

"Learned what?"

"That sometimes it's okay to lie."

"What are you talking about? I never said that."

"No, but lots of times I watched you make up

things to get what you want."

Bruce felt as if he'd been hit. He thought back to the "stories" he'd told while he was looking for Milton's father, pretending to be someone he wasn't. But those "lies" were necessary. If he hadn't told them, he wouldn't have gotten the information, and without the information, they wouldn't have found William.

"It's not okay to lie, Carly. But sometimes it's necessary to tell stories in order to get what you need. We had to find William, and making up those stories was the only way I knew to do that."

Carly clicked her pincers together. "So if I need something, and I lie to get it, that's okay."

"No," Bruce said, sighing. "You can't lie just to get what you want. It has to be really important."

"So if I think it's really important, then it's okay to lie."

Bruce felt like he was sinking into a hole and didn't know how to get out. He knew lying was wrong, and Carly was right: he did it a lot. Bruce's expression grew dark. "Finish gathering those mushrooms so we can get back to Agatha. We'll talk about this later."

Carly flicked her tail and took a pile of mushrooms back to Lilly. Bruce followed with his own pile. When they'd climbed onto her back, Lilly ran to where Milton was rolling the mud ball in the stream.

"The mud is getting softer, and Dad thinks he'll be able to push through it soon," Milton said. He still looked worried, but not quite as much as before.

"We're going back to the competition. Stay here with your dad. I think the best idea is to meet back at your home after the competition is over."

Milton looked relieved. "That sounds good, but be careful. I know what Agatha said, and I think she's telling the truth, but it doesn't pay to be careless. Okay?"

Bruce nodded, thinking about what Carly had said, and that it was difficult to know if anyone was telling the truth.

Lilly ferried her passengers back to the hall. She remained outside while the others rejoined Agatha, who was pacing back and forth, stopping to stare into the stew pot each time she passed it. When she saw Bruce and the others come in, Agatha jumped into the air, which was quite a sight. She waved for them to come quickly, and they hurried toward her cooking station.

"How many mushrooms did you find? Do you prepare them first or just toss them in?" Agatha looked rattled, which Bruce thought was probably not a usual condition.

He described the steps in his mother's recipe and tried to keep the mantis calm. Agatha had placed some large pods beside the stew pot, so that her helpers could stand on top of them and help with the preparation. Bruce climbed onto one of them and watched the contents bubbling gently.

"Just drop them in. You can cut them up or leave them whole, but they'll cook fine either way."

Agatha instructed Arthur, her young helper, to add the mushrooms. He climbed onto another pod and began dropping them, one by one, into the mixture. Bruce hoped he hadn't forgotten anything, and also that Agatha had followed his instructions correctly

158

while he'd been gathering the mushrooms.

Bruce looked at the other chefs to see how their meals were progressing. It wouldn't be long before the officials would call an end to the preparation stage of the competition and the judging would begin. Most of the other chefs also seemed nervous, but the smells in the room were wonderful, so Bruce thought the competition might be tough.

After the mixture had cooked for a while, Agatha dipped a spoon in and stirred it. She brought the spoon out and took a taste, holding her eyes shut as she studied the flavor. She stood motionless for a long time. Bruce became concerned. Did the stew taste bad? Had he forgotten something about the recipe? Did she hate it? Why was she so silent?

"This recipe . . ." Agatha opened her eyes slowly. Bruce's stomach churned. She fixed him in her gaze. "This recipe is fantastic! Oh, I am ecstatic! It will be a win for sure—the crowning glory of my already impressive repertoire. Bruce, thank you for the start of a completely new career with meals that don't require live elements!"

She reached out, grabbed Bruce, and lifted him high off the ground. Bruce was terrified. Maybe Milton was right with his warning. Maybe Agatha had forgotten her oath and planned to eat him. If not, what was she doing? She brought him up in front of her, and he cringed, expecting her to bite off his head. He thought it strange that he noticed her eyes were not single eyes at all, but rather very large groups of many little ones. Instead of examining further, however, he shut his own eyes and prepared to die.

When he felt her mandibles touch the side of his face, he knew it was over. But then Agatha's mouthparts touched his other cheek, leaving a bit of moisture behind, and he realized that she had simply given him kisses. She put him down, clapped her forefeet together, smiling, and went back to stirring the stew.

Bruce shivered. He was still getting over this scare when a bell clanged, and a large cicada beetle wearing a funny-looking hat made an amazingly shrill sound that could be heard all over the large room.

"What does a rabbit use to keep his fur in place?" Henry whispered. Before anyone could answer, he said, "Hare spray!" To his credit, Henry managed to hold his stink in. Even Bruce had been very startled by the loudness of the cicada's call.

"Cooking is done," the beetle called into a megaphone so everyone could hear his voice. "Put down your cooking tools, and stand back from your stations."

All of the chefs and their helpers moved away from the simmering pot. Bruce was nervous, and he was sure that Agatha must feel the same. He looked at his friends. Carly was gazing at the crowd. He thought she looked hungry—like she had when they found her and she tried to poke him. He was hungry, too— his stomach rumbled, as it often did, and the smells in the hall made that worse. He wondered if only judges could sample the dishes, or if those in the hall could taste them as well. Henry looked excited, too, and Bruce hoped this was for Agatha's sake and not because he felt anxious. Bruce didn't want to ruin

Agatha's chance at success by having Henry add an undesired odor to her main dish.

"Thank you, chefs!" the cicada said, removing his hat and sweeping it in front of him as he bowed. With a flourish, he swept the hat back onto his head and turned in a circle until he faced the audience. "Welcome, everyone, to our annual cooking competition! Each year, chefs and those aspiring to become chefs gather from all over to take part in this wonderful event. As you know, we have limited the participation in this contest to insects and animals who are the size of a rat or smaller." He again indicated the creatures on the stage. "Larger animals have their own competitions, of course, but none quite as wonderful as this one!"

Bruce looked over the crowd and realized that he didn't see any caterpillars or butterflies. In fact, quite a few species were missing altogether. He wondered why they weren't included.

As if reading his thoughts, the beetle turned his way and said, "We hope to have even more participation next year, and we're doing our best to spread the word about this glorious contest so that other insect species, along with bats, birds, and other creatures who may not even realize this competition exists will show up and bring their greatest recipes . . ."

"Get on with it!" hissed a small snake from offstage. "They're falling asleep!"

"Well, I don't want that," the cicada said, not looking bothered in the least, "but it's important that . . ."

"Call the judges!" the snake said, and this was repeated by others on the stage, which started a chant that the audience shouted, too.

"Call the judges! Call the judges!"

"Fine, fine," the cicada said. He motioned for five creatures who were seated at the side of the stage to come toward him. A small turtle, a salamander, a dragonfly, a bee, and a toad made their way to the center of the stage. The cicada introduced them, stating their credentials and generally being very long winded. Bruce realized how tired he was. It had been a very long day, with so much excitement, and now, with the cicada droning on, he wanted very much to take a nap. He sat down on the floor and leaned against the pod to rest for a little while, at least until the beetle finished the introductions. He was awakened from the nap he hadn't meant to take when something sharp poked him in the back. He looked up and saw Carly shaking her head and tucking her stinger back into a curl. He decided to concentrate on his rumbling stomach in order to stay awake.

"And now, without further ado—judges, begin sampling the dishes. Please mark comments on your cards secretly—don't share your information with the other judges. Return here when you've finished. I will collect the cards, and my colleagues—he indicated the snake and some others off in the wings—will tally the results and declare the winner."

The judges, who didn't look very awake themselves, ambled off in different directions. They tasted each dish, sometimes twice, made comments on their small cards, and then moved to the next competitor. The first judge to sample Agatha's stew was the toad. Agatha spooned out a large bowl of the mixture and set it on a small table with a spoon. The toad didn't bother with the spoon—he lapped the stew directly. Agatha wrinkled her face and looked perturbed as she clicked her forefeet together. The toad finished lapping, licked his lips, and wrote on his card. He looked at Agatha and said, "Thank you," before moving on to the next chef.

The other judges followed, each sampling her stew and making notes, until all had returned to center stage. They gave their notes to the cicada, who in turn gave them to a very large mouse, who ran offstage with them, followed by the snake.

"It shouldn't be long now, competitors and friends," the cicada said, and he was right—it was only short while before the mouse appeared with a single folded card in her paw.

"Have the judges made a decision?" the cicada asked the mouse.

"Yes, they have," squeaked the mouse, whose voice seemed very high and thin for a mouse of her size. She passed the card to the cicada who held it without doing anything.

"Open it!" sighed the snake, who had slithered in behind both of them. "We should have been done with this competition ages ago. This is taking so long, I'll have to shed my skin again soon."

Unflustered, the cicada opened the card and read its message. He folded the card again and turned sideways so he could speak to the competitors and the audience at the same time.

"As most of you know, in previous years, we have awarded trophies to the competitors who received votes, starting with those who earned the least and ending with the winner who received the most. This year, we have an unprecedented event." He paused for effect, but began speaking again when it appeared the snake might bite him. "We will award only one trophy this year, since only one competitor received all of the judges' votes."

A surge of voices began in the hall.

"Please bring the first-place trophy," the cicada said, and the mouse appeared, carrying a hollowed-out acorn that had been beautifully polished and mounted on a pedestal. "Engraved on the side of this trophy are the words, 'Master Chef, Winner of the Island Cooking Competition.'"

The cicada turned and began walking toward the competitors. He started to Agatha's right, moving in front of the mud wasp, and then he headed further back, passing the field mouse and the tree frog. He continued toward the gerbil, the lizard, the rat, the field mouse, the finch, and the tarantula, until he reached Agatha's station.

"Miss Agatha Moss—you have received the judges' highest honor. Please accept my best wishes and this trophy. You are the winner of this year's cooking competition!"

The hall broke into an uproar. Hats flew into the air, and insects and animals cheered. Some of the other chefs looked disappointed, but each, in turn, came forward to congratulate Agatha and pat her on the back.

"If that trophy is too heavy for you, Agatha, I'll be happy to carry it back to my house," the tarantula said with a smile.

"No, you don't!" Agatha said. "This one goes home with me and will be displayed for everyone to see. But all of you were fine competitors. You had me worried this year. Trying something new, I wasn't sure if I would soar or fail."

"Looks like you're soaring to me," exclaimed the finch. "And I didn't think mantises could fly that well!"

The cicada made another of his shrill sounds, and the commotion in the hall settled down. "This competition is now over, but please feel welcome to come up on stage and meet our fine chefs, our wonderful competitors. With that, I bid you good day!"

"I'll be having a better day now that that overgrown pill bug is done talking," Carly said.

"Me, too," Henry said. "Why did the mother clam scold her children?"

Carly looked at Henry and narrowed her eyes. "Those riddles are ridiculous."

"Yes, but you smile when I tell them," Henry said.

"I'm not smiling. I'm grimacing."

Henry looked hurt and turned away, pretending to be interested in the crowd that had assembled around Agatha.

Bruce poked Carly, who shook her head. "Ask him," Bruce whispered to her so that Henry couldn't hear. Carly closed her eyes and shook her head again. "Ask him, or you realize we'll be right back where we were, and he'll be stinking all the time." Bruce gave Carly a nudge.

Carly opened her eyes and looked at Bruce with a

pleading expression, but finally she sighed.

"Henry—I don't know. Why did the mother clam scold her children?"

Looking pleased, Henry turned back to Carly and said, "Because they were being shellfish."

Carly groaned and Bruce winced. Henry beamed and wiggled, reveling in the joy he always got from his own humor.

Chapter 23

Back to Milton's

"I can tell you one thing: if I never see mud again, it will be too soon. I'm staying inside from now on when it rains!"

Bruce and the others laughed in sympathy with William, who was still recovering from his ordeal in the mud ball.

"I'm glad you're back, muddy or not," Milton's mother said. "I was so worried!"

"Fiona, it will take more than mud to keep me away from you, my dear." William took hold of Fiona's midsection, swept her into the air, and twirled in circles with her above him.

"William! Stop that!" she cried, although she was smiling. When he set her down, the young spiders cheered.

This reminded Bruce of the times when his parents would fly out in the late afternoon, just before dusk. They flew so close that their wings almost touched each other, beating in unison. Sometimes they flew in circles, trying to see who could go fastest and catch up to the other one. He loved it when they showed how much they loved one another, because it made him feel warm inside.

That reminded him of the story about the day

they flew together and found his egg, and that led to thinking about his egg parents again.

He wasn't sure he wanted to find them anymore. Ever since Carly mentioned that they might have abandoned his egg on purpose, Bruce thought it might be best to forget the whole thing and go home. Even if he continued looking, he knew he couldn't trust Conrad, who was a liar. Bruce wasn't sure he wanted to ask the great owl to help him now, either, and he was angry that Conrad sent them on a life-threatening journey that never needed to happen.

Of course, if they hadn't gone to the island, they wouldn't have been able to find William when he was taken . . .

Things were very confusing. Maybe he and Milton should just stay here enjoying Milton's family. Bruce did enjoy being with them—it was so different from being an "only caterpillar." Then, when it seemed time, he would go home again. To his old home. His only home.

Bruce was startled when two hairy legs covered his eyes, and Milton's voice said, "Guess who?"

"Don't you know who you are?" Bruce smiled.

Milton removed his legs. "You look like you're lost somewhere else, somewhere serious. Do you want to leave?"

Bruce looked at his friend. He knew that Milton would agree to go, right now, if he decided it was time, and he knew again that Milton was an incredible friend. "No, let's stay here a while longer. There's no rush. Agatha said she wasn't going anywhere after she went home from the competition, so we don't have to worry about that."

"It was amazing that she agreed to try your recipe. It was even more amazing that the recipe won! No, wait—I didn't mean—I didn't mean that I didn't think your Mum's recipe might not be good enough to—I meant—aw, you know what I mean," Milton said, blushing.

"I know," Bruce said, smiling again. "I thought it was great when Agatha said she was going to start a new cookbook with recipes that don't need any insects or animals as the main ingredient. I like that."

"My Dad would agree with you," Milton said, and they both laughed. "Being in that mud ball doesn't seem to have hurt him. I can't believe how hungry he was after we got him out of it, though, and I thought he'd never stop drinking the water from the stream."

"I guess he hadn't had anything to eat or drink for a long time. You know, we were pretty lucky to find him and get him out of there in time."

"Lucky in general, and lucky to have you to think of ways to do things and solutions to problems. You always amaze me with your ability to come up with good ideas."

"We were lucky," Bruce said, gazing into the forest. The light was fading and soon it would be dark. This time of day always made him uneasy. He always found himself looking around, trying to determine if the shapes he saw were simply leaves in the trees or something else, and listening for the sound of leathery wings on the wind. All seemed quiet. Of course, there was so much noise coming from Milton's home, that it would have been hard to hear a bear crashing through the woods.

"Bruce, there you go with that faraway look again. Are you sure you don't want to leave?"

"We'll go when we know your Dad is completely recovered and when you've had enough of being here. Besides, you don't have to go back with me, you know. This is your home. If you want to stay here, I've still got traveling companions with Henry and Carly and Lilly."

It was Milton's turn to become lost in thought. "I didn't even consider that," he said. He watched his brothers and sisters laughing and chatting with their father. "I do enjoy being here. It's familiar—it's where I grew up. It's home. There are lots of memories and, of course, I love my family." He was quiet, watching as the little spiders jumped up and down and bounced over their father. "But if I stayed here, I would miss the things you and I have left to do together. I don't know why I relish being caught by evil bats and the like, but I do enjoy our adventures, and I wouldn't have any of that if I stay. Besides, I can always come back, now that I know about the island."

Bruce worked to swallow the lump that had formed in his throat. "Let's go back and join the party, before some evil bat catches us out here," he said. "Race you!" he said with a grin, and Milton laughed.

Chapter 24

Lilly Finds a Friend

The travelers stayed at Milton's home for two more days before Milton said he was ready to leave. Bruce had spent a lot of time thinking about family, parents, lies, and truths. While part of him wanted to get back at Conrad for what he'd done—to deceive him, perhaps, or trick him in some way—Bruce had decided that his only reason to return there would be to explain to the great owl that Conrad had lied. He didn't plan on asking the great owl for any information.

Milton's mother gave them hugs, Milton's father patted them goodbye, and they piled on top of Lilly once more.

It was midday when they reached the place where they'd left the other rescued animals after leaving the boat. Bruce wondered where they'd gone—the bobcat, the parrots, the fox, and Eugene—and how they were doing on their own.

The travelers climbed down to give Lilly a chance to rest. Bruce watched the docks and the boats that were tied there. He thought he saw the same boat that had brought them to the island in about the same spot it had been before. He wasn't looking forward to the trip back—the first one had been very long and scary when the fire broke out. He hoped they wouldn't have another storm on the way back.

After a while, Bruce turned to ask Lilly if she was ready to go. She was gazing intently toward the park near the docks. Quite a few humans were there with children and some small dogs. The humans were feeding the wild birds, and the dogs were chasing each other and playing with the children.

Lilly sighed.

"What's the matter, Lilly?" Bruce asked.

"Nothing," she answered, looking away.

"It's not nothing. I can see that you're sad. What's wrong?"

"No, it's nothing, or at least it's nothing I can do anything about. You remember when I said I wanted to know the taste of freedom?"

Bruce nodded.

"After being with you and being "free," I know now that I'd be happier if I lived with a little girl like one of those over there. They look like they are having so much fun with their dogs. I want to do that, too." She turned away from the view of the park and gazed down the road.

Bruce watched the children tossing balls and the dogs who chased them. He could see how that might be fun, if you were a dog.

"Lilly, why don't you go over there and adopt a girl?"

Lilly turned and stared at Bruce. "You mean, just choose one and stay with her?"

"Well, I don't know the proper way to do it, but, yes—why not?"

Lilly looked at the children again, but then she shook her head. "No, I should help you get back to the mainland safely."

"You've done enough," Bruce said. "You saved us from the rats, and you helped us go everywhere we needed to go. You've been so very good to us. Now it's time for you to do something for yourself."

Milton moved behind Bruce, and he also nodded. "We can make our way from here. After all, we got from Bruce's home to the boat the first time, so we can get there again. Besides, we're older and tougher now."

Lilly laughed, because Milton was doing pushups to show off his strength.

"I don't know," she said, looking back at the park. "What if the children don't want me?"

"Then you can come back with us. But why not try?"

Lilly paused, appearing to think it over. She closed her eyes and stayed that way for a few moments, almost as if she were making a wish. Bruce thought that might be exactly what she was doing.

She opened her eyes and said, "You're right, as usual, my friends." She stretched out her paw and Bruce touched the tip of it with his forefeet.

"We will miss you, Lilly," Milton said.

"I'll miss you most," Carly said, making a face, "because these bugs are going to want to ride on me now."

Lilly looked over at the children again, took a deep breath, and sighed. "I'll miss you, too. You've been wonderful friends. Have safe travels. Wish me luck!"

"Good luck!" Henry said, buzzing after her as she darted away and down the path toward the park. Bruce watched her disappear behind some bushes.

A little while later, he saw a young boy and girl arrive at the park with their mother. The little boy and his mother went to play on the grass. The little girl sat on a bench, playing with her doll. Lilly crept out from behind the bushes and darted beneath the bench where the girl sat. She moved carefully, so as not to scare the child, and rubbed against the little girl's leg.

Bruce saw the girl look down and then reach out to pet Lilly. The ferret raised her head toward the girl's hand. A few moments later, Lilly jumped to the seat and crawled into the little girl's lap.

The girl called out to her mother, who turned around, and saw her daughter petting her new friend. Obviously startled, the mother took the little boy by the hand and ran toward the girl. It appeared that she realized the ferret was not hurting her, and she and the little boy also sat and petted the ferret.

Bruce watched as the little girl and her mother talked. The girl hugged Lilly to her chest, and finally the mother nodded. Bruce hoped that meant that they would be taking Lilly home with them. He found a lump growing in this throat, knowing how much Lilly had struggled with her decision to give up her freedom and seek the companionship and love of a human child. He was happy she found her path and proud that she'd had the courage to see it through.

He looked at the rest of his friends. Milton and Carly were still watching Lilly. He was about to ask if they were ready to go, when Carly spoke.

"Looks like Lilly found her freedom. She found the freedom to choose her own kind of life."

Bruce wondered how a scorpion as young as Carly managed to have such wisdom.

Chapter 25

Back to the Mainland

The boat trip back to the mainland was far less eventful than the first one. Bruce, Henry, and Carly spent much of their time hidden away, safely lodged in a cupboard in the back of the galley. This hiding place allowed them easy access to scraps of vegetables, meat, and other leavings that the cook didn't clean up.

The boat's cat, Horatio, was their largest problem. He spent much of his time around the galley, also hoping for a tidbit or scrap. Since the cook was not good at picking up after himself, Horatio ate well, as his ample figure would attest.

But Horatio usually left the galley during mid-morning and again in mid-afternoon when the meals were done and preparation for the next meal hadn't yet begun. The cook was usually gone at these times, too, either napping in his bunk or sitting on the deck when the sun was out. Milton would peek down from the cupboard and, when he was sure the cat and cook were gone, the friends would climb down and begin feasting on the leavings.

Today, there were lettuce leaves and celery tops, along with bits of fruit and flakes of grain. Bruce liked the celery tops, and he also enjoyed a tuft from the top of a carrot which had ferny edges. Henry enjoyed the stems of leftover spinach that the cook had used for last night's soup.

Milton and Carly spent more time searching for their meals. Neither of them much liked the meat scraps that were available, preferring instead to find live meals. Carly's favorite food so far on this trip had been a small cricket, which caused her to become quite happy, at least for a short while. Milton found several grubs which he shared with Carly, and he found no shortage of flies.

The days had a kind of lazy rhythm, with the comings and goings of the cat and the cook, then foraging and feasting, and back to the cupboard. Bruce was glad for the time to rest and think. He tried not to imagine what lay in store once they landed, but it was hard not to think about making the trip back to Agatha's home and then onward to Conrad. Bruce told himself it wasn't important to find out about his egg parents. He hadn't known about them the whole time he was growing up, and he could keep it that way. His parents loved him, and he loved them.

But what would he become? Was he a moth? How many times had he asked himself that question on this trip?

He forced himself to think of other things. He thought back to their last adventure, and into his mind came images of Meryl and Angie, Sophie and Julia, and, of course, Stang. Angie had said she'd seen Samson carrying Stang's lifeless body across the field. He couldn't have survived, just as Meryl had not survived. Even now, at certain times, Bruce felt deep pangs of loss when he thought about Meryl. She was his first real friend—a friend who loved him for himself, and who would help him no matter what. A friend who died trying to save him. His heart ached.

He thought about Milton, his other great friend. Bruce wondered if he was as good a friend to Milton as Meryl had been to him. He frowned, thinking the answer was no, at least on this trip. The times when they had nearly been killed had been his fault for chasing after a selfish goal that never needed to happen.

"You're going to wear a hole in the wood, if you keep pacing like that," Carly said. Bruce had been so lost in thought he hadn't noticed that she'd climbed up to the cupboard and stood behind him.

He stopped pacing and lay down on some bits of sacking and shredded paper. He sighed.

"That's a large sigh for a fairly small caterpillar."

"I am not small. In fact, I'm quite large for my age."

"Compared to most things, you're small. So why the big sigh?"

Bruce didn't want to talk about what he was thinking and feeling, especially not to Carly. She spoke her mind too freely, and he didn't want her advice. He said nothing.

"Okay, fine. You change your mind, let me know."

Bruce turned over to face the wall. If he couldn't pace to get rid of his feelings and thoughts, perhaps he could sleep and shut them out.

He had dozed off when Milton returned. "Good news! The shore is in sight, and we'll be stopping soon."

Bruce turned over, rubbed his eyes, and sat up. He wished he felt as happy as his friend. Perhaps if he acted happy, he would begin to feel that way. There was no way to know what was going to happen until it happened, right? He began to understand that plans were fine when you were in control of what was happening. In this case, too many things were beyond his grasp. He would just have to wait and see how everything unfolded.

Having come to this thought made him feel as if a large weight had been lifted from his shoulders. Then he flinched when Milton did a somersault and landed next to him.

"I am going to get you for that," Bruce said, and he took off after Milton, who jumped down out of the cupboard, trailing a dragline after him, and landed on the counter below.

They hadn't seen or heard the cook return to the galley, but the cook was quick to spot the large spider that landed in front of him. His hand flew out and smacked the counter, but Milton dodged to one side and dropped to the ground.

Bruce couldn't see him any more. He'd watched the whole thing and wasn't sure whether or not Milton was hurt. He couldn't do anything until the cook left the kitchen, and that wouldn't happen for a long time. Preparations for the evening meal were just beginning.

Then Bruce remembered Henry squirting Agatha at the theater. "Henry—can you fly down there and spray your stink at the cook?"

"Sure!" Henry said, and he flew out of the cupboard. He traveled in a circle around the cook's head and then flew straight by his ear. When Henry's backside was just beyond the cook's nose, the little bug let go of a large stink. The cook's hands flew to his face and the flour he'd been carrying flew everywhere.

"Aaauuugh!" he cried, rushing to the sink. He splashed water onto his face and into his eyes, trying to remove the burning liquid.

Bruce crept down Milton's dragline as fast as he could, hoping to reach the floor before the cook came back to the counter. He made it below the edge of the counter before the cook reached for a towel.

He dropped to the floor as soon as he thought it would be safe. He looked all around, but he couldn't see Milton anywhere. As he moved around the base of the counter, he spotted the cat—and Horatio was looking directly at him.

Bruce froze, thinking about his best chance of escape, trying to remember if there were any hiding places behind him, all the while keeping his eyes on the cat. Horatio stalked toward him.

Bruce backed up, thinking that he'd seen a gap in the wood at the base of the counter. He thought he might be getting close to it when two long, hairy arms grabbed him from behind and dragged him into darkness.

"No need to get yourself killed on my account," Milton said, still pulling Bruce backward. Suddenly, a black, furry paw poked through the gap and swept around, slashing at the air. Bruce scrambled back even more quickly, dodging the cat's sharp claws.

"Certainly not," Bruce said, trying to catch his breath.

Milton let Bruce go and turned to look at him. "Glad Horatio didn't catch you. I'd hate to have you come to save me, and then me have to save you, and so on and so on. That would get tiresome after a while."

Bruce looked at Milton, who didn't even have a smile, but then he cracked up and they both began to laugh. They laughed so hard, the cat became enraged and thrashed his paw around wildly.

"Oh, my stomach," Bruce said, rolling on the floor. Milton laughed harder, which brought on a new wave of giggles from them both. When they didn't have any more laughs left, they both lay there, Bruce on his side, and Milton on his back with his legs bent so the tips were touching his abdomen.

Horatio must have grown tired of swiping under the counter, because his paw was gone. When they'd been quiet for a while, Milton said, "Thanks for coming after me."

Bruce looked at his friend and a warmth filled his heart. "That's what friends do."

Chapter 26

Visiting Agatha

After the boat docked, they made their way to the pier using the ropes again. All in all, Bruce thought, the trip back had been fairly easy, but perhaps he was just glad that no great emergencies had arisen.

As they headed toward Agatha's home, Bruce noticed that the leaves were beginning to change colors. He knew this meant cooler weather was coming, but for now, it was beautiful. The sun still warmed them, even as the wind blew the leaves around in circles on the ground. Bruce liked it especially when the wind picked up the leaf he was standing on and blew it across the ground.

They reached Agatha's tree by mid-afternoon. Bruce didn't want to climb up without being invited. That would be risky, considering she might not realize who they were and... well, he felt it would be better to announce their presence. As they neared the tree, they heard a voice humming and singing a lighthearted tune from above. It had to be Agatha. He hadn't thought of her as the type who would enjoy singing—she seemed so gruff and difficult during their encounters at the competition. Bruce wondered if perhaps she had a visitor.

"Hello, Agatha," he called loudly. No response. Bruce called again a few more times. When she still didn't acknowledge them, he suggested they all call together. Just when he thought Agatha probably couldn't hear them over her singing, he heard a rattle and a banging followed by a crash, some muttering, and finally, "Oh, dear, hang on! I'll be out in a minute." Bruce recognized Agatha's voice, but it had a different quality—a softer, higher tone—and she sounded—well, happy.

There was a little more banging, but eventually Agatha emerged from her space inside the tree and stood outside on a branch. She wore a white apron that covered the front of her from her neck almost to the ends of her forelegs, and she wore a lopsided chef's hat on her head. When she saw the travelers, she threw her forelegs wide open, and a large smile lit up her face.

"Welcome, all of you! I've been waiting for you to arrive. Oh, do come up and sample some of the goodies I prepared for your visit. I wasn't sure when you would get here, so I've been baking for days, ever since I got back. You must be tired from your travels. Come up and rest. I have some extra rooms where you can leave your things, if you wish. Come, come! Don't be afraid. I extend my hospitality and give you my word that you will be safe while you are here."

Bruce hadn't expected this. He had assumed it would be difficult to get Agatha to want to help him, even though she had agreed to do it. He had even wondered if she would go back on her word.

In a whisper, Bruce asked Milton, "Do you think it's safe?"

183

"Well, she gave her word."

"She probably isn't too hungry anyway, if she's been doing all that baking," Henry said.

"If she tries anything, she'll be sorry. I'll sting her!" Carly said, giving her fiercest look. From such a small scorpion, it looked quite funny, and it was all Bruce could do not to laugh.

"After you, then," Bruce said, bowing to Milton.

"Oh, no, I insist. After you," Milton replied, gesturing with his foreleg up the tree trunk.

Bruce took a deep breath, in and out, and started up the trunk of the tree, followed by Carly, and Milton brought up the rear. Henry flew up, staying close to the others, and settled on Milton's head when they reached the branch where Agatha stood.

Bruce extended his forefeet to Agatha in a gesture of friendship, but Agatha opened her forelegs and threw them around Bruce. Unlike when she kissed him at the competition, he wasn't terrified this time, but he still found it disconcerting to have something as large and deadly as the mantis showering him with affection.

Agatha's embrace happened so quickly that even Milton didn't have time to react, and Carly was still closing in with her stinger over her back. Henry let out a stink, and it was all Agatha and the other travelers could do to keep their eyes open.

"Oh, dear, I've startled you. I'm sorry," Agatha said, shaking her head. "I didn't think... well, no matter. I wanted to thank you properly for all that you've done for me."

Bruce stepped back a little. "What do you mean,

'all that you've done for me'?"

"For helping me win the competition, of course, but more than that. You started me on a completely new way of cooking. I gained a great deal from you that day. If it hadn't been for you, I probably would have won the competition—I usually do, you know—but this year's win was far greater because I—or you, your mother, and I—have begun a new era in cooking. The competition will never be the same. I have convinced the officials that next year only dishes free of insect or animal components will be accepted. It's wonderful. Everyone was amazed at the taste of my—er, our dish, and I can't thank you enough. All the other insects are asking for my new recipes. I'm trying all sorts of new things. It's wonderful, and it's all because of you. Oh, I have a thank you note here somewhere that I want you to give to your mother." Agatha turned and leaned inside the opening of her home. Bruce could see her backside moving back and forth as she rummaged about. Turning around, she gave a note to Bruce.

"Your mum will be happy to have that," Milton said, bouncing up and down. "Imagine! Her recipe won the cooking competition!"

"Oh, yes! Does she know yet?" Agatha said.

"Uh, no, not yet," Bruce said. He wondered if his mother would be happy that he had shared her favorite recipe with Agatha. He hoped she would like the fact that it was a winning dish.

"You must tell her," Agatha said. "It's quite an honor, I think. Of course, I'm sure my preparation helped to give it a fine taste, and I added a couple more ingredients, which may have livened it up a bit.

I copied my version in the note for her. Perhaps one day, I'll be able to meet her and thank her personally."

"She would like that," Bruce said.

Agatha beckoned for them to come inside. They followed her into a small area within a hollow of the tree where she had made her home. She had a large cooking area lined with stones and bits of clay. Around the rest of the room were pillows and pieces of artwork—drawings and small sculptures— that she had collected as prizes for her cooking accomplishments. She urged the companions to relax while she bustled in her cooking area. When she came back, she brought many goodies for them to try. There were tarts made from peaches and dandelion leaves, a honey almond pudding, mushroom and pine nut soup, and two types of salads. Bruce's mouth watered as he looked over the food, and his stomach rumbled.

"See? Not one of these dishes has an insect in any part of it." Agatha beamed.

"But I like eating insects," Carly said, pouting. Seeing the look on Bruce's face, she reddened a little and said, "Well, I do, but I guess I'll try the soup."

Bruce nodded. "I'll try one of the tarts, please."

"The honey almond pudding sounds wonderful," Milton said.

"What about you, my aromatic friend?" Agatha said to Henry.

Henry blushed and said, "What did the bee name his son?" Without waiting for anyone to reply, he said, "Buzz!" and then rose up in the air and began zooming happily around the room. When he settled down again on one of the pillows, he said, "I'll try a little salad, please, if some of the leaves have stems."

"Certainly!" Agatha said, still smiling. She served their food and took a dish of soup for herself. Bruce thought the food was delicious, and he knew that his mother would love to try some of these recipes. Everyone complimented Agatha on her cooking, and she glowed.

When they finished eating, Agatha cleared away the remnants. The travelers looked rested and happy.

"Agatha, that was wonderful," Bruce said, patting his stomach, which was full and fat for the first time in ages.

"Most definitely the best I've ever had," Milton agreed, as he stood and passed the acorn bowl that held the last bits of his pudding back to Agatha.

Bruce looked at Carly, who raised her eyes to the ceiling.

"The soup was okay," she said.

Bruce scowled at her, and Carly made a face. "Yeah, okay. It was pretty good."

Agatha smiled. "I'm glad you liked it. But I know you didn't come here just to eat my food. Bruce, you said you wanted my help with something." She straightened her hat, which had tipped over and was covering her eyes. "I'm still waiting to find out what I'm in for."

Bruce wasn't sure how to begin, so he decided it was best to tell Agatha the whole story, starting with his parents telling him about finding his egg and going forward from there. When he'd finished, with Milton adding comments to round out the story, Agatha leaned back and rubbed her forefeet together.

"That is quite a tale!" Agatha strode to the shelf where she'd placed her cookbook and the new trophy from the competition. She picked up the cookbook and brought it to Bruce, setting it next to him. "I don't need this anymore. I am giving it to you, and you can do with it what you wish. No, I'm certain," she said, as Bruce started to protest. "I don't need it, because I'm beginning my new cookbook. I already have the first recipe (with your mother's permission): a variation on her stew that is the best I've ever tasted, and the other recipes will be experiments with meals that need no meat or insects. I'm quite excited—I'm sure it will be my best work yet. No one will care about the old recipes any longer, so that cookbook will have little value once the new one is complete. Give it to the owl, if you wish, so he will give you the information you seek. It's up to you."

"I—I don't know what to say." Bruce couldn't believe that Agatha was just giving him the book, and he might get the information about his egg parents after all. That is, if Conrad wasn't lying and the great owl really did know something. "Thank you doesn't seem like enough, but it's the best I can do."

"You're welcome, my small friend, and thank you is more than enough. The more I think about it, I would like to come visit sometime. I could meet your parents and talk with your mother about her recipes and learn how she prepares her meals. You'll have to leave me the directions to your home so that I can find it."

Bruce tried to imagine the looks on his parents' faces when he told them that a praying mantis would be coming to visit. He giggled involuntarily. "I will.

I'm sure my mother would enjoy talking with you, too."

"Well, you must stay here tonight. You can start on your way in the morning. Then you'll be refreshed, and you can take with you some of the goodies I'm going to make for you tonight!"

Bruce liked that idea. He wondered how they were going to carry all of the things it appeared Agatha was going to send with them—but they could figure that out in the morning.

Chapter 27

Back to Stony Ridge

After numerous goodbyes and kisses from Agatha, the travelers were on their way. Agatha suggested they make a litter to carry the cookbook and the assortment of delights she'd prepared for them. By using Milton's silk to lash some leaves to two long twigs, they created a platform that Milton could pull behind him. The idea worked quite well.

The morning was sunny but cold. Carly seemed impervious to changes in temperature. She had more than doubled her size since she'd been with them, and her body had developed a thick outer plating. Bruce thought that might be what kept her warm. He stamped his feet as they walked along, and Henry rode behind Milton's head, burrowing into his fur. Although they wanted to stay under cover of the trees as much as possible, occasionally Bruce would stop in a patch of sunshine to get warm. Milton and Henry enjoyed that, too.

Around mid-morning, they passed the small cave where they'd first met Henry.

"I'll never forget the look on your face when you thought I'd made that smell," Bruce said.

"Well, I knew I hadn't done it. Who'd have believed such a little bug could make that enormous stink?"

"Who are you calling 'little'?"

They continued recounting stories of Henry's stinking episodes, including the ones that had helped them get out of terrible predicaments. Bruce was glad that Henry could giggle about it now. He knew the little bug was also growing up and was glad Henry had learned how to control his odor, at least some of the time.

Like the boat ride, this leg of the journey was easier than it had been in the other direction. Perhaps because of the cold and not wanting to dawdle, they made good time. When they stopped for the evening, they were not far from the owl's oak tree. Milton found a spot near the trunk of a small tree that looked like a good resting place. He strung his line around their camp to warn them of predators again. As he finished, the late afternoon sun had gone behind the trees, and dusk was settling in. Milton had just finished his circle and had jumped inside of it, when he felt a tug on the line. Turning quickly, he saw a mouse standing in the shadows.

"Greetings. Remember me? I'm Josie, the mouse whose life you saved before you left on your journey so long ago. I've been waiting for you to return."

"We're glad that you survived," Milton said.

"As am I," Josie said, smiling. "I told you I wouldn't forget your kindness. I owe you my life. But I've come not only to thank you again. I need to tell you what I know about the owl, since I believe you'll be going back to see him. May I join you?"

Milton told Josie to jump over the silken line. Bruce saw the scar on her side where they'd used Milton's silk to bind her wound. It had healed well, and he was proud that Milton's idea had worked.

"We plan to visit the great owl in the morning," Milton said.

Josie snorted. "I've lived around here all my life, and I can tell you that I've never seen any great 'Owl at Stony Ridge.' The only owl around here is Conrad—the little one you met. I heard that Conrad began spreading stories about a great old owl in order to keep himself safe. I guess he figured big creatures would avoid this place for fear of being eaten by a big owl. The legends spread and grew, and travelers began seeking the counsel of the 'wise old owl,' braving the danger to come here when the need for information was great. They arrived, as you did, bringing gifts and offerings. Conrad loved that, so he encouraged the stories, telling those who sought counsel that he was helping while the owl was busy with another matter. Of course, the great owl is always busy somewhere else, because he doesn't exist."

Bruce tried to make sense of what the mouse had said. There was no great owl from Stony Ridge. Even that was a lie.

"While we were gone, we learned that Conrad lied to us," Bruce said. "He sent us to bring back a book that he said belonged to the great owl, but in fact we were stealing it. We planned to come back and tell the great owl about Conrad's lie—I thought he should know what Conrad had done. But now you say there is no great owl..."

"I'm sorry I couldn't tell you before you left. I called out to you, but my voice was too weak, and you didn't hear me."

Bruce began pacing. "I don't know what Conrad planned to do with the cookbook, but it doesn't matter. I'll never give it to him now. I wish I could get back at him for what he did to us. I believed him, and he's nothing but a liar who used us to get something he wanted." Bruce had walked around the circle and turned to pace the other way.

"Looks like you might be a liar soon, too."

Bruce stopped pacing and scowled. "Carly, you don't know anything about it!"

"What I don't know is why you find it so hard to see the truth." She scooted toward Bruce so that he would have to look at her. "You made a bargain. You agreed to bring the cookbook to Conrad. It doesn't matter whether or not he lied. You have the book, and now you have choices. You could avoid Conrad altogether, or you can lie and tell him you couldn't find the book. But neither of those choices are honest ones."

Bruce turned away from the scorpion and began pacing again.

"The only honorable choice is to take the book to Conrad," Carly continued. "Maybe he'll give you the information you hoped for. If he does, then you're better off. If not, you've lost nothing but time, and you've gained new friends. Oh, and Milton found his home, we saved his father from certain death, and we all learned a lot."

Bruce was still scowling. He stopped pacing and stared into the clearing. Carly walked up behind him and touched his shoulder. He spun around, an angry look on his face. Before he could say anything, she held up her claw. "You said I don't know anything, but I've learned a lot by watching you. I know we're defined by the choices we make, and I know the owl can have no effect on you unless you become like he is. Is that what you want?"

Bruce's gaze shifted to Milton and Henry. He wished they'd never found Carly or brought her with them on this journey. He wanted to pick her up and . . . He took a step back, and his eyes opened wide. He looked at Carly and thought about the owl and how angry he felt right now. He remembered the times when he was so angry at Duncan Trumbull who used to beat him up. All he could think of then was finding a way to get back at Duncan. In a way, this was the same: Conrad had bullied them, and Bruce had wanted to do the same to him.

Carly was right.

He hung his head. When he finally looked up, he spoke slowly and quietly. "I hate to admit it, but you're right, Carly, and I know the rest of you agree." He shook his head. "I have no idea how you learned so much in such a short time. However it happened, I need to say thanks for having the courage to stand up to me and say what you think."

The little scorpion flicked her tail. "My pleasure," she said, with a gleam in her eye. "Of course, you know I love telling people what I think."

"I know," Bruce said, grimacing.

"If we're settled, I'm going to get some sleep. All this thinking has made me tired," Carly said, walking away and curling up near the tree trunk.

"May I stay here with you tonight?" Josie asked.

"Of course," Milton said. He was smiling, and Bruce was glad his friend seemed happy again. Without warning, a great yawn overtook Bruce.

"I'll take first watch," Henry said, buzzing in a circle over Bruce's head. "I'm not tired, and some of you," he said, circling closer to Bruce who was yawning again, "need your beauty sleep."

Chapter 28

The Recipe for Truth

As tired as he was, Bruce found it hard to stay asleep. All of them had covered up with leaves for warmth during the night, and Bruce had been comfortable, tucked close to the trunk of a tree, despite the wind and cold. He didn't want to leave his warm little "nest," but he was too restless to lie still any longer.

It wasn't as cold this morning as it had been, probably because of the light fog that lay close to the ground. The dampness covered everything, and, as he walked around the camp, his feet became wet. He stood on his back legs and drank some moisture from one of the leaves. The dew was cool as it trickled down his throat.

Bruce paced around the silken circle Milton had made. As it grew lighter, he watched his sleeping companions. He couldn't see Henry, but he knew the little bug was there, either hidden beneath the leaves or just camouflaged, since his coloring matched them so well. Carly was curled in a small circle next to the tree trunk. Josie had covered herself with a large pile of leaves, but Milton's pile was nearly as big, and Bruce could just see the top of the spider's head. As he moved closer, he realized Milton was awake and looking at him.

"Can't sleep?" the spider whispered. He pushed the leaves away and began stretching his legs, one by one.

"No. Too many things on my mind, I guess."

"I thought you'd settled everything last night," Milton said, moving away from his sleeping companions. "Still not sure what to do?"

"No, I'm sure of that. I'm not making any plans, except to give Conrad the book and tell him we know about his lie. No, it's not that." Bruce scuffed mud from his feet as he walked toward Milton at the edge of the circle. "I can't tell you how many times I've felt bad about one thing or another on this journey. First there was the way I treated my parents when we left home. Then I was so focused on learning about my egg parents that I got us into danger by searching for the cookbook. Later, I didn't want to stop and see your family. I wanted to keep going, and I asked you to leave, even though I knew you wanted to stay. I started to come to my senses after we started looking for your dad and then went back to your home, but I've been really awful on this whole trip."

"Yep, you've been pretty awful, all right."

Bruce looked up in surprise.

Milton tried to keep a serious face but couldn't. "What? You were hoping I'd say it's okay, I forgive you, and you shouldn't worry about it?"

Bruce's face reddened.

"You don't need my forgiveness or approval. You ought to know by now that I accept you the way you are." Milton raised a foreleg and poked his friend.

"Maybe you should, too."

"Good advice," Carly said, as she uncurled and stood. "More good advice would be to let your friends sleep, but no hope of that, it seems."

"It's time to get up anyway, Carly," Milton said. "I'll wake Henry and Josie. We should be going soon."

Carly stretched and walked over to Bruce. "On the subject of forgiveness, I want to—"

"Carly, this isn't a good time," Bruce said, backing away. "We have to get ready to go see Conrad." He turned and started walking toward the others.

"Wait."

"Carly—"

"It won't take long."

Bruce sighed. Carly had a way of piercing inside of him, making him dredge up feelings and ideas that seemed too big to handle. He was tired, and he didn't want to think about things he didn't have answers for right now. He also knew she wouldn't let it go. "What is it?"

"I've thought a lot about what you said when we were gathering mushrooms." Bruce looked pained and started to interrupt, but Carly shook her head and continued. "I understand the difference between the kind of lie Conrad told, when he said the cookbook was his, and your lie at the competition, when you told Agatha's helper that she'd sent you to get William." Carly poked the ground with one of her pincers. "It was the same when you told the centipede and the rat that we were Agatha's helpers, so we could get into the competition. Now I understand why you did it. I'm learning that lots of things aren't as simple as

I thought they were." She looked at Bruce, her eyes wide. "Now I think there are times when it's okay to "tell stories," but it's also important to remember that those "stories" are really lies, and to know that when you tell them. Does that seem right?"

Bruce thought of the time he lied to his parents about where he'd gone, and another time when he fibbed about what he'd done. He recalled the time he told Mr. Willoughby that he hurt himself falling out of a tree, when it was really Duncan who beat him up. Sometimes he did those things because he thought they wouldn't approve, or he didn't want to be punished. He'd lied at school, telling the other caterpillars about things he'd done that had never happened. Of course, he'd fibbed to his Aunt Bess so as not to hurt her feelings, saying he liked her honey cakes when they really tasted terrible.

He'd even fibbed to his mother about his reasons for this trip, saying it wasn't just to find his egg parents, but also to help Milton find his family. Milton did want to go home, but that wasn't Bruce's reason for making the trip. Yet saying that to his mother made his reason for going seem less selfish.

He'd even lied to himself. It was true that he wanted to find his egg parents, and he wanted to know what he would become. But he realized that part of his reason for leaving home was also because he was angry at his parents. He wanted to hurt them like they had hurt him by lying to him all those years.

Bruce closed his eyes, forcing his thoughts to stop. When he opened them again, Carly was still gazing at him, waiting for his reply.

"I won't lie to you," Bruce said, which made him smile just a little, but then became serious again. "I don't have a good answer. I've given a lot of thought to our conversation, too. You're right—it's good to realize when we lie, because sometimes we do it without thinking. I would tell those stories again, in order to rescue William, and I'll keep telling my Aunt Bess that her honey cakes are good, even though they're awful. But I'm going to be more careful about lying to others—my friends, my parents, and myself."

Carly started to speak again, when Milton somersaulted into the air and landed right next to both of them.

"Come on, you two. If we're going to get to the owl before we're too old to care, we ought to eat some food and get going."

Bruce and Henry found some leaves they both liked not far from the tree where they'd camped. Carly, Milton, and Josie went off in different directions, and all returned not long after. While he waited for the others to get ready, Milton cleaned his face with his forelegs, and Josie washed her face with her paws, paying special attention to her whiskers.

When they were ready, Bruce put on his backpack, Milton picked up the litter, and they began the trip to the huge oak where the tiny owl made his home.

The moved slowly through the clearing. Milton kept watch above and behind. Henry, who sat on the litter behind Milton, looked from side to side, and Carly and Bruce watched what was ahead and periodically looked up at the great tree before them. When they reached the base of the tree, Milton set the litter down, and Henry took to the air, flying in little circles over their heads.

"Why did the tree stay home from school?" Henry's voice sounded very high, and Bruce realized the little bug was afraid again.

"Oh, not again," Carly groaned. "I thought he was over that."

"Have some sympathy. Henry's been doing very well," Milton said.

"I don't know, Henry," Bruce said. "Why did the tree stay home from school?"

Henry buzzed as his circles became smaller. "Because it was a sycamore. Get it? Sick-a-more."

"Ugh. I hate riddles," Carly said. "Henry, can't you do something else instead?"

"Stop it, you two, and Henry, calm down." Bruce said. He looked up into the tree and called out, "Hello, Conrad. We've come back to talk with you."

There was no response. Bruce thought perhaps the owl was still asleep, as he'd been the first time they came to see him. Bruce called more loudly.

"Hellooo, Conrad. Hello ... We brought your cookbook."

There was an odd sound, followed by Conrad's voice, saying, "I'm a little busy at the moment ... I'll be with ..."

The owl stopped speaking, and they heard a gagging sound. Without warning, a large object fell in front of them, rolled, and settled near a mushroom. Bruce recognized it as an owl pellet, which meant Conrad had eaten recently—a good sign. The falling pellet was too much for Henry, however, who let out a terrible stink. Bruce and the others tried to keep their eyes open with only partial success.

"Oh, Henry! That's awful! Did you run out of riddles?" Carly asked.

Bruce was worried that the owl might take offense at the smell. "Conrad, I'm sorry about the odor."

"No need," Conrad replied. "Owls don't have a sense of smell, so I didn't notice a thing. Anyway, I feel much better now that I got rid of that pellet. Hope everyone down there is all right. You say you brought the book? Where is it? I'm coming down."

Conrad left his high perch and flew to the low branch where they'd last seen him. He spotted the litter and the book lying on it.

"Is that the book?" he asked. "How exciting!"

"Yes, we brought it back for you. But of course you recognize it, don't you?" Bruce said, unable to keep from taunting the bird.

Conrad fluffed his feathers. "Of course I do. You've done well. May I have it now?"

Bruce still felt sad that he was going to give the book to this owl who didn't deserve it. Milton lifted the book from the litter and dropped it on the ground well behind them. Conrad swooped down, picked up the book in his small talons, and flew back to the branch. Henry let out another small stink, and everyone groaned.

"I'm so sorry," Henry said, settling down onto Milton's head.

The owl placed the book in the crook of a branch and used one toe to open the cover. He flipped a few pages and looked satisfied.

"Wonderful! The great owl will never know it was missing."

"That's true, he won't," Josie said, surprising everyone by speaking. "That's because there is no great owl. There's only you—a tiny, pipsqueak of an owl. You've lied about the great owl from Stony Ridge for years."

Conrad ruffled his feathers again and stared at the mouse with a look only a predator can give. The mouse shrank back, but then stood tall once more. Bruce knew how scared she must be—he was frightened also.

"You have no idea what you're talking about, mouse. I'd watch out, if I were you. When the great owl gets back—"

"Nothing will happen," Bruce said. "The mouse is right. There's no great owl. We know you made him up. We also know the cookbook doesn't belong to you, and you sent us to steal it from Agatha Moss. I don't know why you want her book, but it doesn't matter." Bruce glanced at Carly. "I agreed to bring it in exchange for information. You have the book. Now I expect you to follow through with your part of our bargain." Bruce thought he sounded much tougher than he felt. He hoped the owl thought so, too.

Conrad fixed Bruce with the same stare he'd given the mouse a moment before. "So you think you know the truth? You don't understand at all."

"I understand you're a liar," Bruce said. "Soon I'll know if you're a cheat, too. Do you have the information you promised me?"

The owl fluffed his feathers. "Not yet. I need a little—"

"As I thought. Well, I lived up to my part of the bargain. You can live with the fact that you didn't. Oh, one more thing. Don't ever attack this mouse again. If you do and we hear about it, we'll tell everyone we meet that there isn't any great owl from Stony Ridge."

Conrad turned his head away and closed his eyes. Bruce picked up his pack, preparing to leave, when Carly spoke.

"Mr. Owl—I have a question."

The travelers looked at Carly, who stared at the small owl, waiting for him to acknowledge her.

Conrad turned his head around slowly, opened his eyes, and fixed Carly in his gaze.

"Why didn't you just ask Agatha to share her recipes?"

Conrad's eyes opened wide. There was a long silence. "It never occurred to me," he said. "I didn't think she'd say yes."

Carly looked at Bruce and then back at the owl. "So you lied because you thought the truth wouldn't get what you wanted."

"But you were wrong," Bruce said. "Agatha sent her book with us to give to you. I hope you enjoy her recipes." He put on his backpack and began walking away, hoping Carly and the others would follow him. He was still very afraid of the owl. He'd only taken a few steps when he called over his shoulder, "Remember what I said about the mouse."

"Wait," Conrad said. "I did ask some of the creatures who've lived here for a long time about your egg and your egg parents. Several of them said a huge storm came around the time your egg would have been made. The heavy winds and rain killed many creatures, and they thought your egg might have been blown to where your parents found it. The storm came from the direction of the woods beyond the river. If you go that way and ask, you may learn more."

Bruce turned and looked at the little owl. He hadn't expected any information, and he didn't trust what Conrad had just told him, but still it was something. He gave the owl a small nod and looked at his friends.

"Josie—I wish you good health and long life."

"I wish the same to all of you." She bowed slightly and scurried away through the clearing.

Milton picked up the litter, and they retraced their path toward the trees, back the way they'd come originally.

"I forgot something," Conrad called. He swooped into the air and landed on top of a bush near them. "An old friend of yours was here just before you got back. He told me some stories about your adventures in the cave, and about how you are heroes. He said to be on the lookout, as he'll find you soon. He said his name is Stang."

The Bruce and Friends Books

Bruce and the Road to Courage

Bruce and the Road to Honesty

Bruce and the Road to Justice

Bruce and the Murder in the Marsh

Other Works by Gale Leach

*The Art of Pickleball: Techniques and Strategies
for Everyone*

Short stories and poems included in
Avondale Inkslingers: An Anthology
and
Inkslingers 2013: Memoirs of the Southwest

Visit
www.galeleach.com
to learn more about these books
and others in the works.